The Hideaway

Jennie Cordner

To my dearest husband, David - thank you for taking me to the White Lady Falls, which provided me with inspiration to write this romance.

Chapter 1

Life throws us challenges when we least expect them. To be honest, I thought I'd had my share. However, fate had other ideas. I suddenly lost a job I loved, as a travel photographer, and a man I believed would one day become my husband. That's when I reluctantly made the decision to come home. Sadly, it wouldn't be the last time that I crossed the Atlantic in search of love.

Back in England, my brother, Aiden, offered to put me up, but I had to get used to being on my own at some stage. The ideal solution came with a rented cottage on the outskirts of a small town, close by. Aiden came over to stay for a few days to help me settle in, but before he left he offered some stern advice.

"Please Abbie, stop thinking about your lost love in New Jersey! You're wasting your time, dreaming about the past. Just get on with your life. Learn from it."

Aiden was frustrated by my need to go over and over what had happened and my need for an explanation as to why Mike, my boyfriend, my boss, fired me.

"Get out there, take a break, go somewhere different, see new sights," said Aiden. "You of all people know that you have to get on with life or it passes by. For goodness sake, get into a decent routine instead of moping around."

Aiden couldn't stand to see me so miserable. He believed hiding myself away wasn't at all helpful. As always, he was probably right. I needed a focus. The idea of taking photos in a completely different area proved tempting. For starters, my portfolio required updating to boost my chances of finding work. A regular income had become more important of late. Yes, I had savings, but that was for something permanent, a house to settle into, the forever home.

The holiday cottage in the small advertisement looked very attractive. Set in a tranquil rural setting, not far from the coast, it seemed an ideal place to forget my problems; those areas in my life impossible to solve. As for Bailey, my Northern Inuit, he loved going to new areas with all their different scents and places to explore. He was my constant companion, affectionate and loyal, simply my best friend. When I spoke to him, he listened attentively to my every word, his head cocked to one side, an outstretched paw asking to be held. We had a real connection. He never let me down. His wild wolf-like appearance contradicted with his somewhat cowardly nature, but I just adored him.

Aiden was thrilled when I told him about the holiday cottage, saying he looked forward to hearing all about my stay. "Do you good to see what a different area has to offer. Remember, you talked of going there before you embarked on that ill-fated jaunt overseas! So, take plenty of photos."

"Then I can bore you to death when I get back. Looking forward to it already."

I packed a couple of outfits, two bottles of wine, cheese and crackers plus, food and extra treats for Bailey, into a holdall. With my camera, books and notepads, I had everything I needed. The idea of eating out, savouring the local delicacies and relaxing and indulging myself suddenly looked an ideal way to while away a long weekend.

Aiden came to see me off; probably to make sure I hadn't cancelled.

"Is that it?" he queried, when I dragged my bag into the hall. "One holdall?"

"One *large,* heavy, holdall! Anyway, I'm only going for a few days. You know me; less is more!" I replied.

"Do I really know you Abbie? I'm not sure I do. Anyway, come on, you need to get going or it will be dark before you even get there."

"OK, OK. And don't forget to get my letters in the post."

"Will do. Now, go! I've set your satnav, so just follow the instructions. Stay with it Abbie, then you won't get lost."

"Big brother still looking out for me," I replied sheepishly, coaxing Bailey into the back seat. "But, I'm pleased you came to see me off. Glad to know someone cares."

"And, I always will. You might be this well-travelled businesswoman, but honestly, you are simply useless at times. Please, just take some time out. Go walking. Breathe in the sea air. Relax!" With that, Aiden dumped my holdall in the boot of my car, before hugging me tightly.

"I'll get in touch at some point. Promise. And when I get back we can make arrangements to meet up on a more regular basis. I've actually missed our chats," I said, smiling.

The car exhaust blew noisily in fanfare. Driving away, I had a lump in my throat and watery eyes. Looking in the rear view mirror, waving frantically out of the car window, I watched Aiden retreat into the house. My brother was a real treasure. When I jaunted off wasting all that time in the States I had missed him. Now, he provided me with much needed comfort and common sense. Both single, apart from elderly Aunt Bella, our dearly beloved late father's sister, we only had each other. As for Aunt Bella, I longed to be more like her. She wore clothes that made her stand out in the crowd, whereas I tended to blend into nothingness these days, to go unnoticed, ghost-like. Aunt Bella loved the scent of adventure. When one of her letters arrived in the post, I always made myself a coffee and got myself comfortable, ready to be entertained. I longed to have such fascinating stories to share.

Aiden, he was the total opposite of our Aunt. He was sensible and organised and thought things through before making decisions. I fell between them both, attempting to be carefree whilst making plans. I failed miserably. Take my recent experience for example. I accepted a job overseas, organised my move and it had all resulted in failure. To make matters worse, the thought of this one manipulative man living across the Atlantic still held me back from moving on.

Bailey stirred and gave a whimper, then a sigh. I was sure he could read my mind. If he could talk, he would have shouted, "Enough is enough!" For Mike and Bailey were never the best of buddies. I remembered how Mike liked to stroll through Wissahickon Valley Park in Philadelphia without, '*the hindrance of a dog who stops and sniffs every few steps.*' Even the dog beach was out of bounds. Bailey's pleasures consisted of long walks and swimming in the creek, but Mike refused to understand, raising his eyes heavenwards as he breathed out slowly through pursed lips. (Lips that pressed against mine with eager tenderness in the heat of the moment, yet spoke with such coolness when he said goodbye.)

Bailey gave another sigh, reminding me, I was supposed to be looking forward instead of attempting to manage or rearrange the past. I looked in the rear-view mirror. "Ok, Bailey, time to concentrate on where we're heading," I said, attempting a smile, before turning the radio up. Then, tapping on the steering wheel to the rhythm of the beat, I immersed myself in the English countryside that I had missed so much. It was a real pleasure driving my old classic car again on country roads. Compared to driving my Dodge minivan down five lane highways in the States, roads that seemed to stretch to the horizon, heading nowhere, a joy. Now, twists and turns almost caught me out, but around every corner lay a new scene to enjoy.

Spring, and Nature was in the midst of renewal. Through trees, shafts of sunshine glinted, tempting leaf buds to unfurl from their dormancy. On the wayside, clusters of pale, yellow primroses waved in the breeze, peeking out between fresh fronds of fringed cow parsley. In fields, pregnant ewes made the most of being outside. Soon they would be brought in, ready for lambing. Farmers had busy days and even longer, sleepless nights ahead. I actually envied the idea of being so occupied that I didn't have time to reflect on anything to do with Philadelphia.

Shaking my head, I thought about the next few days. Of dawdling down quiet lanes to my heart's content before snuggling up with Bailey on a comfy sofa in front of an open fire, a good book on my lap and a glass of red wine on the table. But first, I had to get to the cottage. I seemed to have been driving for hours, but looking at the satnav my destination was still some way off. My shoulders ached and the back of my neck felt tight. I needed a drink and a bite to eat to keep me going. At the next junction, I branched off into a small village where a quaint cottage beckoned me over with a sign outside advertising Cream Teas. It was just what I needed.

An aroma of baked goods wafted towards me as I opened the door. My tummy rumbled. The teashop looked quintessentially English with blue and white gingham tablecloths and a pine dresser stacked with pretty, floral china. On a long trestle table, draped with a lace tablecloth, scrumptious looking fairy cakes, scones, a Victoria sponge and a chocolate gateau, jostled for my attention. A young woman, wearing a Cath Kidston vintage style pinafore darted in from the kitchen to take my order. She told me I had got there just in time, as in another fifteen minutes or so she would be shutting up shop. I hurriedly decided on a fruit scone. Spread with homemade strawberry jam and a huge dollop of clotted cream, it was simply delicious. To wash it down, I sipped tea from a china teacup, hand painted with pretty wild flowers round the bowl and on the saucer. I even remembered to hold my little pinkie out as I drank!

Afterwards, I took Bailey for a short walk down the lane before he happily leapt back into the car, where he took up the whole length of the back seat.

"Right, ready for the off, my handsome boy?" I asked, bowing to kiss his silky muzzle, telling him I didn't need a wash as he licked my face all over. He answered with a swift, excited wag of his bushy tail and gave a snort, before settling back down on his tartan blanket.

"Well, here we go, Bailey. At least I haven't got us lost, yet," I chuckled, despite the fact Aiden always said I had difficulty finding my way out of a car park.

However, the strangest thing happened when I turned the satnav back on. It started speaking with an American accent. That threw me for a moment, as it seemed so odd. Perhaps, I'd pressed some button or other by mistake. Still, as long as it got us to our destination, I didn't really care if it spoke in Japanese. After all, the route map hadn't changed. So, shrugging my shoulders, puzzled but not overly bothered, I fastened my seat belt and headed off.

On the hour I listened to the news, mostly doom and gloom. I tried not to dwell on it, pressing the button for the CD player instead. Frank Sinatra was one of my all time favourite singers. I happily sang along until I reached the line, 'when I was thirty-five, it was a very good year'...that stopped me dead. Last year, I was thirty-five and it had not been a good year at all. I waited for the next song to begin. But when Frank Sinatra began to croon, 'hello young lovers', his voice warm and full of meaning, my eyes misted over.

It was *our* song; the first song that Mike and I had danced to. Memories came flooding back, instantly.

Last year, Mike asked me to join him at his father's house for Thanksgiving, the traditional holiday sandwiched between Halloween and Christmas. I regarded the invitation as something special. First, we joined thousands of spectators lining the streets of Philadelphia, to watch Macy's Thanksgiving parade. It marked the unofficial kick-off to the holiday season and featured floats and giant balloons, live music from stage shows, various street performers, plus of course Santa. Like youngsters, we enjoyed it all. Then, we set off to Mike's family home for our meal.

The large Colonial mansion stood at the end of a long sweeping drive. An avenue of trees sparkled with shimmering fairy lights. My eyes stood on stalks when the house finally came into view. Of huge proportions, it looked amazing and so elegant. The heavy, front door was decorated with swags of greenery, red bows and shiny baubles. Wreaths suspended by wide, red ribbons hung down in front of all the shuttered windows. There was a beautiful sleigh packed with display gifts on the front lawn. Lit icicles dangled down all along the guttering. Lanterns lead the way up stone steps towards a life-sized Santa sat in a rocking chair by the door. Overboard, perhaps, but the child in me loved it.

Inside the house, the spacious hall was ablaze with crimson poinsettias. At the foot of the curved oak staircase, a huge Christmas tree stood proud. It almost touched the ceiling. From the living room wafted the scent of pine, cinnamon and cloves, plus something to settle my nerves, the rich, sweet smell of prepared eggnog!

Mike's father, a widower, introduced me to his lady companion, Barbara. They shared holidays and social occasions, but not his home. Mike Snr was someone who liked the space to himself. He made all the decisions about his home. Barbara suited this arrangement. Good-natured, she took delight in giving me recipes for the splendid feast we shared; roast turkey, sweet potatoes, mash, grits, green beans and bacon, followed by pumpkin pie, the classic desert of Thanksgiving. Afterwards, both tired and happy, Mike and I said our goodbyes. Mike had booked us in at The Rittenhouse Hotel for the night, which stood in one of the most desirable locations in the city. Mike liked privacy too.

In the Library Bar we sipped creative cocktails. Mike seemed very relaxed. He held my hand and entwined his fingers in mine. His eyes studied my face, and looking puzzled, he asked me if something was wrong. I just smiled, stroked his arm and shook my head. But, after three long months in this relationship, this would be the first time we had actually spent the whole night together. We had both wanted to take things slowly. Mike said he had been hurt in the past and I had my own reasons. So, till now, at the end of each date, we always went our separate ways - Mike to his place in the suburbs and me to my apartment in town. Tonight, anticipating a full, rounded relationship I had something important to tell him. I kept going over in my mind how to begin. To save any embarrassment, I had decided to wait until we were on our own.

"If you are anxious about tonight, I'm nervous too! But, tonight will be whatever you want it to be. Don't look so worried. It's not your first time, is it?" he teased.

What could I say? Yes, actually it is, at least the first time since my operation. The thought of baring my body made me blush. I was scarred and scared.

"We, I mean I, need to talk. Not here. Let's go to our room."

Our suite was opulent and beautifully appointed. Full-length windows gave us a view of Rittenhouse Square, the fountain and sculptures. It was impressive. As I stood gazing at the scene, feeling nauseous, Mike came and stood behind me and encircled me in his arms. Then, he kissed my cheek and playfully nibbled my ear.

"So, what did you want to tell me?" he whispered.

I turned to face him. "Something I should have mentioned a long time ago."

Mike looked puzzled. I kissed his hands and said he had better sit down.

"There's something you need to know about me. I'm sorry that I never told you before, but I didn't want it to be the first thing you knew about me. I was worried you'd back off without giving me a chance."

"What are you saying Abbie? This is all so weird."

When I told him, two years before coming to America, I had surgery for breast cancer, his eyes flickered and a startled expression came over his face. He shook his head, looked down at his hands, coughed and then let out a huge sigh.

"Why now?"

"Because, I wanted you to get to know me first, without that preconception of me as, you know, different. And if my disclosure ends our relationship, so be it. I had to walk this long road to accept myself as I am, but if you can't do that, I will understand."

Mike shrugged his shoulders. "Whatever happened to you is in the past," he said. "Please, Abbie, I don't need to know more."

I still wanted to explain.

"I've had a mastectomy," I said, quietly.

Mike stared at my chest, shook his head and before I uttered another word, put his finger to his lips and shushed me. To him, it was history. He closed the conversation telling me it made no difference to how he felt about 'us.' My story, a chapter in my book, he didn't want to read, at all. In fact, he stumbled repeating the word, *cancer*.

Confused and self-conscious, I simply commentated on the wonderful view, before reaching for my glass of wine.

Mike smiled. "Here's to our future," he said, holding his glass aloft.

"The future," I repeated, stunned that he still cared enough to even think of a future with me in it, without a full explanation. Physically, I was different now and there was so much more besides. Perhaps in a day or two he'd allow me time to say more.

We clinked our glasses together before I emptied mine in one long gulp.

Mike smiled and took our empty glasses and placed them on a tray. He acted as if I hadn't made any disclosure at all. Smiling, he beckoned me to stand, bowed and invited me to dance. Almost in a trance, my head fuzzy with wine, I slipped between his arms quite readily. My relief was palpable. Held in a tight embrace, I felt pretty special. Soon, I was snuggling into his chest, my heart quickening with the warmth of his body. In the background, Frank Sinatra sang, 'Hello young lovers.' When the song ended, Mike held me at arm's length and looked at me intently, with desire. That night we became lovers. Too eager to wait for me to get fully undressed, sex was rushed, which at the time only made me feel incredibly wanted. Now, I was anything but! Still, as Aiden kept insisting, no use dwelling on the past.

I wished Aiden had come with me for the weekend. We always enjoyed each other's company, relaxing, sharing a bottle of wine or, reminiscing about our happy childhood. Those memories gladdened my heart. Growing up, we didn't have much, but we knew contentment. Living in the countryside on a smallholding gave us such freedom to roam and get close to nature too. As long as we came straight home from the fields when Mother sounded the hunting horn, a signal that dinner was on the table, our parents never worried. During the long, hot summers, we practically lived outside. Tonight, a soak in the bath before relaxing in front of the fire with a good book was on the cards, instead of reminiscing. It had been such a long day. Aiden was right. I had left it a bit late setting off.

Ahead, glimpses of the sea nudged against an inky sky streaked with red and gold. As the sun began to slip towards the horizon, I relaxed back in my seat, knowing my journey was almost at an end. I saw crows lining up on telephone wires, congregating before they went to roost, balanced like musical notes on a stave, and I felt ready to nestle down too. But, to re-energise myself, for the last part of my journey I turned the radio back on, full blast. Then, with the windows wound down I sang out loudly, breathing in the salty freshness of the sea, aware that no one could hear me!

My moment of pleasure changed the second I glanced at the satnav. Then pure panic set in. The map had disappeared; the screen was blank, except for an arrow pointing nowhere. Desperate, I reached down and fiddled with the plug, twisting and turning it in its socket, trying to get the satnav to spring back to life. Nothing worked. I wanted to scream.

The country road continued to funnel downwards. With all the twists and turns, I lost all sense of direction. Then high hedges and deep banks closed in, as the road suddenly narrowed. Bailey pressed his nose against the window and whined. I slowed down and pulled over. There was nothing around for miles, just an empty, deserted middle-of-nowhere space. As darkness deepened, a blanket of fear pressed down, clothing me like a shroud.

Chapter 2

Bailey hopped out of the car and joined me. Head down, he snorted through fronds of ferns and leaf mulch on the bank. I peered into the darkness. My heart raced at the sounds of wildlife tunnelling through bracken. As the noises grew louder, Bailey stood rigid, the hackles on his back raised. I got goose bumps too. Within moments Bailey left my side and headed back to the safety of the car. My heart thumped, as I wondered what sort of animal was about to lunge out from the undergrowth. Shaking, I flew round the bonnet of the car and jumped into my seat. "Let's get away from here, now," I stuttered.

My fastened seat belt cut uncomfortably into my shoulder. I didn't waste any time sorting it out. I just wanted to get going. My hands shook and the car keys jangled, as I fought to place them in the ignition. Then, when I turned the key, the engine didn't fire. It just spluttered and coughed until it died. I wanted to weep.

Rifling through the glove box, hunting for a torch, I felt desperate. The situation was dire. However, I soon realised I'd left the torch at home in the shed, when I went outside to leave a spare key in a safe place, under an empty pot. Nothing had passed me for mile upon mile, so it was no use thinking about being rescued. Exasperated, I wondered why my car let me down. Betsey, as I called her, had been in storage during my time in the States. Yet, when I came back from America, I turned the key and her engine had purred without hesitation. So, what had happened now? Betsey, used to belong to my father and memories formed part of my attachment. The idea of abandoning her on the side of the road filled me with guilt. But, what else could I do? I knew nothing about cars. I left all servicing to mechanics. I had heard the terms, flat battery, faulty fuse, and ignition problems, but I had no idea on how to deal with any of it.

The road was narrow and twisty. If by a chance a car came along in the dark it could knock me for six. In the distance, a cluster of lights shone out. I had little choice but to head towards them, in a direct line, over the fields. As I manhandled my holdall out of the boot, Bailey reluctantly joined me. He looked nervous, pleading, his head on one side.

"It will be OK," I told him, kissing the top of his head, before fastening the lead to his collar.

A full moon eased out from behind the clouds, which allowed me to find my way up a steep bank between bushes and trees. Last year's fallen crab apples crunched and squelched underfoot, as twiggy branches reached out to scratch my face like sharp fingernails. Bailey forged on, tugging on his lead. At the edge of the field, he stopped, head up, sniffing the air. His hesitation made me look around and over my shoulder. There was no point going back.

"Off we go boy, soon be there," I said, fearfully.

The grass around the perimeter of the first small field was wet and slippery making the rubber soles on my shoes squelch. But, it became worse when the grass gave way to ploughed earth. Squishing through sodden soil wasn't at all pleasant. By the time I had plodded through the second larger field, I had bumpers of earth stuck to my shoes, weighing me down. Totally exhausted and out of breath, I was thankful when the gate to a small, secluded, timber-clad cottage came into view. My holdall now weighed a ton.

A length of rope tethered an old garden gate to a fence post. After untying it, I struggled to shove the gate open. It protested noisily, as I slammed it shut before making my way down a rough stone path. A smell of wood smoke raised my spirits, as I headed towards the lit building. I shivered at the idea of sitting in front of an open fire, nursing a hot, sweet cup of tea.

Suddenly, Bailey decided to go on ahead, yanking his lead clean out of my hands. I hoped he hadn't picked up an interesting scent to send him off back into the fields; there would be no stopping him. With his long easy stride he covered a lot of ground quickly. Fortunately, he ran in the right direction and was soon hurtling up a set of wooden steps and onto a veranda in front of the cottage. My heart pounded in my chest as I hurried to catch him up. Then, just as I thought everything was going fine, Bailey targeted an upturned bucket and sent it pitching towards a rickety table. They collided with a loud clanking noise, followed by a thud and a rattle as a mug shot off the table and onto the deck. I squeezed my eyes shut, wondering what Bailey would do next. All I heard was Bailey slurping up the spilled drink. When I opened my eyes he was standing next to a wooden crate, looking over his shoulder towards me, his tail wagging from side to side, like a huge, hairy sickle. With an exaggerated movement of his head he beckoned me over, making a low harrumph sound, the same noise he always made when he wanted my space on the sofa!

A paperback lay on the deck, splayed out face down. The title, In the Land of White Death had the tagline, 'an epic story of survival.' Not a bad omen, I hoped. I picked it up and placed it on a chair before righting the bucket and small table, along with the emptied mug. With things back in their place, I stepped towards the door; surprised that no one had ventured out to see the source of all the commotion.

In a wooden crate by the door, lay bundles of kindling. I glanced towards the windows. The curtains were closed. I looked at the sign above the door; '*The Hideaway.*' I imagined going inside and simply disappearing, forever.

I tapped lightly on the door and looked towards the window, expecting the curtains to peal back to reveal a face staring out. Nothing happened. A babble of voices inside made me hesitant to knock again. I stood for a few seconds and then took a deep breath. "Well, here goes," I whispered to Bailey. This time my stronger rat-a-tat-tat brought a result; the unlocked door creaked open. I waited.

"Hi, hi, is there anyone there?" I called cautiously, through the gap in the door. Again, nothing. Then, before I had a chance to stop him, Bailey barged past, fed up waiting for an invitation.

"Bailey, come. Bailey come. Pleeeease!" I pleaded, patting my thigh to encourage him back out. He ignored me and instead lolloped down onto a colourful braided rug in front of a huge inglenook. He looked happy, brushing the mat with his black-tipped tail. A beckoning look on his face said, come on, it's lovely and warm in here. I looked over my shoulder and then back into the house, my heart racing. I had little choice.

I kicked off my filthy, wet shoes and placed them next to a pair of dirty boots on the doormat. Then, leaving the door ajar, I crept in. That's when I realised; the voices came from a radio plonked on an old chest of drawers. There was no one about. I dropped my bag, somewhat relieved.

Bailey rolled over, exposing his belly for me to rub. Then, he let out a deep breath of contentment as he stretched closer to the blazing fire. The draught from the open door blew round my neck so I quietly pushed it to. Glancing round before hunkering down, I was pleasantly surprised. The cottage, albeit, a little ramshackle on the exterior, looked inviting inside. With old, comfy, fireside chairs and a huge wicker basket piled high with hand-knitted throws, it was cosy. A scrubbed table set for one, with a glass of red wine and some fat green olives in a ceramic bowl, created an ordinary scene, which made my heart quieten. I edged closer to the fire, rubbing my hands together, luxuriating in the heat. My hands tingled as they came back to life. It felt so good to be inside and warm, albeit in a stranger's home, certainly, a better alternative to staying in the car with wildlife all around. When the owner returned, I only hoped they'd be friendly. And I prayed I wouldn't have any difficulty finding my way back to my car when it became light. Utterly drained, I closed my eyes for a moment, telling myself this was all part of the adventure, something to tell Aiden and Aunt Bella about!

Bailey nudged me. I leaned over to hold one of his outstretched, muddied paws, thankful that the cottage had hard stone flooring and not some fancy, pale cream shag pile to spoil. No, a fitted carpet wouldn't have suited the room at all. It was full of character with a beamed ceiling and whitewashed walls. Nothing stood out to distract from the overall charm. It didn't appear wrought by years of family living, just simply furnished with lamps on assorted odd tables coupled with a few ornaments, candlesticks and framed photographs; nothing too twee or expensive. In fact, it was the kind of place, in a remote area that I could have done with when I returned from the States. Somewhere, I wouldn't be disturbed, except by the odd fellow who had lost their way!

"Well Bailey, what have I got us into?" I murmured, wondering when the door would open.

An aroma of pipe tobacco hung in the air, reminding me of my granddad. More than likely, whoever lived there was elderly and eccentric, I thought. Pleasant too, I hoped. Still, I had little choice other than to wait and see. I needed a refuge and I had found one. The rest depended on who walked through the door. In the meantime, the open fire was just what I needed on such a cold, dark evening. In fact, the cottage only required a woman's touch to make it perfect.

Either side of the inglenook, pine shelves stacked high with paperbacks and hard backed books showed someone had a passion for reading. They covered every type of genre. As I looked around, a silver framed photograph caught my attention. It showed a young woman, younger than me, perhaps in her twenties, sitting on a beach, leaning against a rock, toes digging into soft sand. She held a large clamshell up to her ear. Her short blond hair bathed in sunlight formed a halo round her head. Everything about that photograph spoke of contentment. It helped to lessen any lingering unease.

Next to a wingback chair stood a longcase clock. The hypnotic movement of the pendulum, the rhythmical tick tock, made my eyelids grow heavy. I didn't wish to be caught off-guard and so I quickly stood up, rolled my shoulders and went to peer out the window. It was drizzling now. We had got here just in time. Not that Bailey minded the wet. Show him a muddy puddle and he would be in it, plastering himself in muck. The same with fox poo! Yes, he was a delightful friend to have at times. But his companionship more than made up for his faults. Best friends like to focus on the positive.

I glanced back to the grandfather clock just as it started to chime. Six thirty. Goodness, was that really the time? I glanced at my watch to double check. Sure enough it was, even though my battle-worn body was struggling to stay awake. I scanned the room, looking for something to do to reinvigorate myself, to stop from falling asleep.

Over by the sink, a tea towel draped over a large earthenware bowl aroused my curiosity. Lifting a corner of the tea towel, I peered inside. The bowl contained a skinned, gutted rabbit. It resembled a premature baby. It made me heave. On the draining board lay a discarded butcher's knife and a soiled rag, soaked in blood. Crimson spots stained the bare floorboards. I kept repeating to myself, it's just a rabbit, just a rabbit, but at the back of my mind, I wondered if we should leave. However, my situation hadn't changed; I was lost, it was cold, it was dark and it was raining. And, I couldn't even call anyone because my phone was in for repair; I didn't think I would need it on my *lovely* weekend away! No wonder my brother called me Dilly Daydream. And the cottage, well it didn't appear to have a phone so there was no way to contact the outside world tonight. I only hoped I had been right to trust Bailey's intuition. After all, he had a good sense of flight or fight and after a quick sniff around he had settled in the cottage, unperturbed. That gave me hope.

I thought my intrusion might be appreciated if I did the bit of washing up in the sink. Occupied, I might stop worrying too. So, half closing my eyes, I carried the earthenware bowl with the naked rabbit over to a scrubbed topped table, asking myself how something fluffy and cuddlesome, ended up looking so repulsive.

Doing the washing up was one thing, but it seemed a bit presumptuous to go nosing about in cupboards to find tea or coffee, though I could have died for a cuppa. My tummy rumbled. I fumbled in my coat pockets. Amongst the loose change and tissues, I found a toffee to chew. Then, I caught sight of myself in the mirror. What a state I looked; nothing like the pretty girl in the photograph, young, lean and carefree. My casual clothes, denim jacket, pink sweater, bobbly round the cuffs and front, jeans, mud splattered and worn, could have come from leftovers at a jumble sale. My hair was tangled and windswept too. My best feature, if I had one, were my eyes, forget-me-not blue with dark sweeping lashes that required no mascara to make them stand out. But, my mouth chomping up and down didn't look very attractive at all. Plus, it reminded me too fiercely of chewing gum and life back in the United States and how I'd got the job there in the first place.

Two years before, I had applied for the position of travel writer and photographer at a company based in Philadelphia. The interview took place via webcam.

For the face-to-face interview I wore a fine, linen business suit and swept my long, dark hair up in a soft chignon, fixed with several pins decorated with tiny glass beads. I believed I'd fully prepared for the interview and yet, nothing equipped me for the actual event.

In front of my computer, I tried to appear calm, in control and professional when really I was a bundle of nerves. Mike, son of the Director, represented the company. He was alarmingly good-looking with hair the colour of polished steel and sapphire blue eyes. His eyes mesmerized and unsettled me. I remember staring at his face. It was perfectly symmetrical. His skin looked silky smooth without a trace of stubble. I could almost sense what it would feel like to run my fingers down the side of his cheek. Holding my gaze with this handsome man on the other side of the Atlantic made me so self-conscious. I must have looked awe-struck.

Mike's father, Mike Johnson Snr hardly helped the situation. Sitting in a corner of Mike's office, he kept leaning forward and whispering in Mike's ear, keeping an eye on me at the same time. He also wrote notes on slips of paper and passed them across the desk for his son to read. My cheeks reddened uncomfortably as Mike scanned the notes before nodding in his father's direction and mouthing, "Yes, Sir."

Mike followed his father's written requests, inviting a lot more detail. My fingers trembled and my palms got all sweaty as the interview progressed. I put my hands in my lap, out of view. In addition to hiding my nervousness, I didn't want Mike or his father to see that I wasn't wearing either an engagement or wedding ring. To me those little accessories showed commitment, which might have an impact on being taken seriously as a candidate for the job. Neither did I wish to come across as some unlovable woman on the other side of the world! Of course now, that's exactly what I was!

That job in America had been my all-time dream. Yes, the work was challenging at times, but visiting places to capture scenes I had only glimpsed in films or glossy magazines before, more than made up for it. From San Diego, San Francisco and the Grand Canyon in the West, to Baltimore and Boston in the East, the assignments offered such superb opportunities. Even so, my all-time favourite place was pretty close to my rented home in the suburbs of Philadelphia. The picturesque landscape of rolling, lush green hills, dotted with little red barns and windmills in Lancaster County, home of the Amish, became somewhere I happily escaped to, whenever I got the chance. It showed a humble life could be very pleasing. On the outside looking in, it seemed so anyway. I made my first visit after reading Plain and Simple, the story of a woman's journey to live with the Amish. It captured the essence of living in the present, in the moment. I envied the simplicity of such a simple, peaceful life.

During my research regarding the Amish, I learnt of their frugality. Having four dresses was more than adequate for Amish women: one for wash, one for wear, one for dress and a spare. Their outer clothes were black, both for men and women. This served as an understatement; so no one stood out as being above any one else by the way they dressed. Their buggies, horse drawn modes of transport, graphite grey in colour, blended in rather than standing out. It was a life of real minimalism. Yet, their handmade quilts, displayed in specialised shops and outside Amish homes contrasted vividly. In rainbow hues, they looked absolutely beautiful. All the different patterns had lovely sounding names, Log Cabin, Tumbling Blocks, Carolina Lily, Garden Maze and the unforgettable, Double Wedding Ring. I purchased a Double Wedding Ring quilt for my bottom drawer! In my mid thirties, ready to settle down, I was feeling hopeful that marriage might come along soon.

The sound of the garden gate slamming wildly against the gatepost instantly brought me back to the present. Bailey rushed straight to the door, his tail wagging furiously in welcome. My heart thumped. As sturdy footsteps pounded across the deck outside, my legs started to shake. I held my breath. The footsteps grew louder as they edged ever closer to the door.

Chapter 3

The door scraped open. My eyes widened in alarm. A man dressed in camouflage gear and army boots filled the doorway. His stance was war-like, his face contorted in pain. From under his hat, blood dribbled down the side of his face and into his beard. His forehead above his left eye was swollen in the shape of a hen's egg, glowing blue and black. In his right hand he was holding a shotgun, an old-fashioned rifle with a long barrel. I stepped back, away from the door. This wasn't the elderly man I had been imagining.

"What the hell…"he said, brusquely, looking none too pleased at finding a stranger in his home. "Suppose, those dirty shoes out there are yours, are they?"

"I'm sorry, but the door was open so I came in. You see my car broke down. I was lost," I rambled.

He scowled and banged the butt of the rifle on the floor, making me jump. Then, he cupped his eye and flinched with pain.

"I've had a bit of an accident," he said, gruffly. I could do with some help." With that he staggered over to a chair, plonked himself down and propped his gun up against the table leg. When he tugged his hat off, I saw a nasty gash on his head. Bailey looked over, whimpering, his earlier exuberance spent. None of us knew what to make of the situation.

"That's my dog, Bailey and I'm Abigail, Abbie," I murmured.

"Well, thanks for the introduction. I'm Bill. But, don't just stand there gawking. Get some water and a cloth and start cleaning me up," he barked, impatiently.

I grabbed a sheet of kitchen roll and handed it over before pouring some cool water into a breakfast bowl. The man, Bill, closed his eyes and I began to gently dab at the wound. But, getting up close to someone I didn't know was awkward to say the least. His warm breath against my face as he winced in pain, the feel of his skin under my fingertips, the intimacy left me silent for a moment or two. As I cleaned the last of the blood away, he suddenly blinked before looking directly at me. Then, I found myself drowning in the most beautiful, hazel eyes I had ever seen. Those windows to the soul showed a real depth of sadness too, however hypnotic.

"Are you trying to mind read?"

Startled, I replied hastily, "Yes, umm, no, what I mean is, I've finished."

He raised an eyebrow, coughed and then smiled before calmly saying, "Well, thank you. Abigail you said?"

"Uh, yes,"

Any trace of a man about to do battle had vanished. I gave a weak smile and briefly looked towards Bailey to stop myself staring. Without the look of pain etched across his face, Bill, was quite handsome, well, more than a bit, very! I fingered strands of my hair, curling them round my fingertips, before firmly tucking them behind my ear, suddenly aware that Bill may have read my signal as one of anxiousness or even flirting!

"About time we had a cup of tea. Unless, you fancy something stronger?" he said, lightening the mood. "Then, you can tell me why you are here."

"Tea would be lovely. Thank you. The reason I'm here is because I got lost. Still, it's lucky I was here to help you," I said, my cheeks reddening.

"Things happen. I'm just a big clumsy fool who tripped over and bashed into a tree. The branch didn't give way, but my forehead did. I never should have attempted to chase that pesky fox that keeps trying to get at my chickens. I've lost two of them recently. Not that I want to harm the bloody animal, but my chickens don't need chasing until they die of exhaustion or fear or have their heads bitten off. That fox needs to have his fun, some place other than in my chicken run!" he said, breathlessly.

"So what will you do about it?" I asked, timidly.

"Don't look so worried. I've finished ranting. I'll strengthen the pen and secure the hen-house. My chickens will be safe then."

"Seems like you are gonna be busy."

"Shouldn't take too long. And sorry I was so gruff. Just annoyed with myself really."

"No worry. I expect finding a stranger in your home was quite a shock?"

Bill laughed, a good hearty laugh. "Yes, not often out here you would happen across someone breaking and entering! Especially someone with a wolf in tow!"

"I didn't," I replied, meekly, "the door was open…"

"That's what they all used to say," Bill replied.

"Look, if it's not too much of a bother, will it be OK if I stay a couple of hours and head off as soon as it's light? Though I might need some direction to find my way back to my car."

"Stay as long as you like. Though, I'm not used to company. In fact, it's been a long time since anyone, apart from the old boy who buys logs from me, has come within miles of this place. An old woman used to live here before me and she spooked the daylights out of everyone. They used to call her a witch and all sorts. But, she was just an old eccentric, someone who wanted to be left alone. I bit like me, I suppose. Anyway, you look pooped. I'll get us something to eat. You can sit and daydream by the fire until it's ready."

"You sure? That's very kind. I did stop and have a bite to eat but that seems hours ago. But, don't let me put you out."

"No problem. I'm ready for something to eat myself any way. Grilled trout ok?"

"Well yes. I wasn't expecting a hot meal!"

"Not exactly. Just fish and homemade bread!"

"Sounds great."

While Bill set to making our meal, I focused on the fire, watching flames leaping and twirling in a rhythmic dance. Yet, all the while, I grew more and more conscious of the young lady in the photograph staring down at me. Even when I crossed the room to place my empty cup in the sink, she seemed to follow me with her eyes. No doubt, my imagination working overtime again. Perhaps, the girl was Bill's daughter. I didn't like to ask. However, she looked nothing like him. She was slim with delicate features and blue eyes.

Bill had a rugged appearance, maybe a little overweight, but someone who you'd enjoy a good cuddle with. Not your bony, super fit look-at-me type. A man of substance not style. Perhaps, the girl took after her mother, I mused.

We ate our supper with plates on our laps in front of the fire. The fish, stuffed with onions, spinach and bacon was grilled to perfection, the skin lovely and crispy. It was so tasty. After we had eaten, Bill excused himself by saying he was going outside to look at the stars. But, the cloud-filled sky meant another shower and so he soon came back in. Then, for the rest of the evening we listened to music on the radio and chatted, not about anything in particular or important, just in a low-key manner. I mentioned that I had never visited the area before. Bill said Devon was a wonderful place to live and the scenery could not be bettered. He talked about Dartmoor in a romantic way, describing the vast moorlands, little villages and deep river valleys with their rich history and rare wildlife. His passion for where he lived spanned back to childhood albeit he had only properly reconnected with it a few years ago. I thought he was lucky to have found his forever place in a landscape he loved.

During breaks in our conversation we both seemed content to let the cracking and spitting of the fire to take over. My imagination made up pictures as sparks settled before they died on the blackened back wall of the hearth. A small flame in the shape of a spirit danced and flickered. The image was comforting.

Bill was happy for me to stay until morning. I felt comfortable in his presence. His manner made me feel safe. He offered me the spare room upstairs, but I took up the alternative suggestion of a makeshift bed on the sofa in the snug. That arrangement suited me better. Bill was a stranger after all, although no doubt he thought exactly the same about me!

It was almost midnight by the time Bill took his bed. Steam rose from his wet and worn jacket, which he left to dry in front of the fire. Bailey stretched out on the rug alongside the sofa. Despite his dense coat he liked to be cosy. Soon, he was snoring his head off, twitching his long limbs, dreaming. For hours, until my eyes ached, I stared up at the beamed ceiling. Mike was still the all-time keeper of my sleep. Thoughts of him went around and around in circles. I tried to rewind different scenes hoping to erase them fully. However, thoughts of that day when everything culminated in devastation stayed fresh in my mind.

Seven months ago, September 23rd to be precise, at ten thirty in the morning, Mike, called me into his office. I thought he was going to brief me about my next assignment. Instead, he announced that my contract and role in the company had come to an end. He barely looked at me as he told me. Not only that, he declared our personal relationship was over too. Open-mouthed, my eyes brimming with tears, I waited for an explanation. He simply dismissed me both as an employee and a girlfriend with some business speak.

"We enjoyed having you with us this past year Abigail, and want to thank you for your dedication to the company. Now, we need to put a new format over to our clients. We need a new Team player."

I shook my head, bewildered. At a recent meeting with his father this hadn't been discussed;

there had been no mention of, *a new format*. As I stood trembling, wondering what on earth I had done wrong, sure that all of my assignments had been within budget and on time, Mike interrupted my thoughts.

"No doubt you will be glad to return to your beloved England, Abigail. But, we shared some good times, didn't we? Pity, we have become incompatible of late."

Incompatible, I wanted to scream. Surely he could have come up with a better excuse to end our connection, both personally and in business terms?

My cheeks blazed. Through my tears I stared blindly back at Mike. He was sitting behind a large, highly polished desk, which served as an island in-between us. He couldn't even look at me. Instead, he looked down at his hands, which were firmly clasped in front of him. Floundering in a sea of complete misery, I thought I was going to throw up. Swallowing hard, I fumbled in my pocket for a hankie. Mike pushed a box of tissues across the desk and gave a little smile. But, any support or salvation was quickly swept aside when he said, "We just might meet again one day. But, for now, I guess its goodbye." His voice was calm and cold, the smile a lie.

I remained sitting for a moment or two, paralysed. Mike stood up and offered me his hand to shake. Stunned, I slowly shook my head. Then, out of the corner of my eye, I glimpsed his father in the adjacent room, looking at us both through the glass divider. His face showed no trace of emotion. Mike always had to put his father first in any matter; he was constantly at his beck and call. It was always a direct,

"Yes Sir!" So, had I been both hired and fired under Mr. Johnson's exact demands? Or, was the reason far more personal?

I stumbled to my workstation as the rest of the department, including Marcia, my so-called friend, carried on with their work. Hands shaking, tears flowing, nose streaming, I gathered my bag and pair of trainers from underneath my desk. Then I scuttled to the door. Mike's eyes burned at my back. In the elevator, my legs shook violently. Like a wounded animal, I struggled to stay upright.

Back in my apartment, I scurried from room to room closing all the blinds. Bailey, must have wondered what on earth was going on when I scrambled under the bedclothes without getting undressed. Pulling a blanket up and over my head, I tried to block everything out. Bailey whined and clawed desperately at the covers. I reached out and patted his head and he soon settled down, nuzzling into me, offering me comfort. Still Mike's words, 'We have become incompatible of late,' kept running through my head.

Deluded with love, I used to make up excuses for Mike's reluctance to spend quality time together. If he forgot a prearranged date, I told myself it was due to work commitments and something must have cropped up last minute. After all, we managed to arrange alternative evenings together so, I didn't need to complain. Ignoring my last birthday? Well, I wasn't a child. Once you reach your mid thirties it's not so important to celebrate every year is it? And anyway, he made up for that by sending me a huge, hand-tied bouquet of flowers. He had it delivered directly to my desk. *'Yes, precisely'*, that voice of reason in my head whispered – '*to the office, so everyone could smile and oh-and-ah saying how special he was.*' Trouble was, I'd expected something different on my birthday that year. Perhaps jewellery or a little velvet box and a man down on one knee! Yes, I was such a pathetic dreamer.

After a month of drowning in sorrow, waiting in vain for Mike to message me, I called my brother and told him I was coming home. Aiden thought I ought to stay. He attempted to reassure me, saying another job would soon come up. He reminded me that the USA was the land of opportunity. However, I just wanted to come home. As for my Aunt, the eternal optimist, she told me not to look on it as failure, but as a lesson learnt; that sometimes a muddied diversion leads to a solid road and future happiness!

The Westminster chimes rang out from the grandfather clock bringing me back to the present. In a few more hours it would be getting light. My best friend had barely stirred all night, except for making little whimpers and soft barks as he contentedly drifted in and out of dreams. He seemed perfectly at home in a strange place. In fact, perfectly at ease! If I got the courage to delete Mike's saved voicemails on my phone, perhaps I'd too find peace. Goodness, how many more times would I listen to them? His New Jur-zee accent, it made my heart melt. When I got home, after this weekend, hopefully reality would overcome all the pretence. Then, with a press of a button, he'd be gone, for good. Then life could become almost normal. With that thought, I found myself finally drifting off to sleep.

I stirred several hours later with Bailey's paws on my chest and his hot breath caressing my face. His weighty body wasn't easy to shift.

"Get off, you big lummox," I moaned, easing myself up.

There was a soft tap on the door. "Got you a cuppa," called Bill. "Shall I bring it in?"

"Yes please," I replied, straightening the covers.

"I'll put it out of reach of the wolf. Take your time. Breakfast isn't quite ready."

"Thanks," I mumbled, rubbing my eyes. "I can't believe that I actually slept."

"It's this cottage. The Hideaway is a special place, somewhere you can dream. Oh, and I had to let Bailey come in with me a couple of hours ago, as he was whining and pawing at the door. Hope you don't mind?"

"I never heard him."

"I'll leave you to it then. Breakfast will be ready when you are," Bill said, smiling. When he headed back to the kitchen, Bailey followed. When I found my special place, I hoped to look as relaxed as Bill. Nothing seemed to really faze him. However, I wasn't sure about welcoming in a stranger with a hound for the night. Bill had been so kind to do that. I needed to find a way to properly thank him.

I stretched and shook the covers off, ready to get moving. In the snug, the air was heavy with the aroma of wood smoke and damp clothes mixed with the unmistakable pong of wet dog. But, from the kitchen wafted the mouth-watering smell of bacon cooking

I eased myself off the couch. The stone floor was freezing under my feet. I slipped my woolly socks on and padded over to the window, sipping my tea. When I drew the curtains back, sunshine poured into the room. I squinted and peered out. My shoes had been moved. Still, they needed a thorough clean and polish after my walk yesterday. Once I got dressed, I would see to them. I patted my hair down into place and smiled on hearing the hum of the kettle on the stove. The shrill whistle signalled another pot of tea! I quickly pulled a pair of slacks on over my pyjamas and headed into the kitchen, rubbing sleepy dust from my eyes.

"About time too!" teased Bill. He tapped his watch. "Some of us have been up for hours! Bailey's been out for a good walk; I've cleaned your shoes and breakfast is almost ready. Hope you fancy a hearty fry up to start the day? I've cooked enough for two."

Bacon and eggs sizzled in a pan and thick slices of brown bread lay buttered on a plate. It had been ages since I had proper bacon, true British, back bacon.

"Umm, it smells wonderful. How can I refuse?" I replied, licking my lips, all at once starving. "Anything I can do?"

"Well, you could make the tea while I finish up and then perhaps you can tell me where you are heading?"

"Might be a problem. You see I left my satnav in the car. It's got the address on it. Plus, it might need charging."

"Satnav? I'm not into all that techno stuff. Give me a map and compass any day."

"Sure. Anyway, perhaps I'll just head back home, that's if I can get my car started. The weekend is almost over now, so that might be best."

"You American? You got a slight drawl, but I can't quite decipher the accent."

"No, but I lived there for a while. But, I hadn't realised I'd picked up an accent. I'm originally from the Cotswolds. Have you heard of Witney, a market town in Oxfordshire?"

"Yes, famous for the Witney blankets that apparently got their softness and quality from the river water used in the manufacturing process," Bill said matter-of-factly.

"Most of the factories are long gone. Time changes everything. Developers have turned the remaining buildings into homes and flats. People like the idea of living in converted industrial buildings, don't they?"

"Lovely area. I called into Witney when I visited Burford, some time ago."

"I went to school in Burford. Fancy that!" I gushed.

"Yes, some coincidence. Anyway, Abigail, don't rush off on my account. Stay here another night. At least you will have had a break and I can show you the White Lady Falls. Yes, my place is rather untidy, but then I wasn't expecting guests, was I? Although it's quite nice having a bit of company for once."

"I'll think about it. Thanks. To start with, I need one of those tasty bacon and egg sarnies if they are ready. And call me Abbie, please."

Bill nodded and gave a ready smile. "Help yourself. Go on, get stuck in!" he said, sliding a plate across the table, before plonking himself down.

"Well, Sleepy Head, glad you got some shut-eye! I didn't. Having to keep an eye on you as well as that blimming fox kept me awake. Anyway, what brought you to this area?"

Wiping my mouth, I told Bill, it was somewhere I had always planned to visit, just that the opportunity had never arisen before. "However, at the moment

I'm job-hunting which has some advantages; time on my hands for instance," I said. "But, tell me more about the White Lady Falls."

"Well, the main source comes from the river Burn. It cascades about a hundred feet into Lydford gorge. That point is known as the elbow of capture. They can't compare to the Niagara Falls, but honestly they are worth seeing. You ought to make the time."

"Well, they do sound interesting. I might get some good shots I suppose," I said, thoughtfully.

"Dartmoor superstition has it that The White Lady Falls is named after a ghost. Others think that when it's in full flow it takes the shape of a bride in a white flowing gown. You would be charmed, I'm sure."

"Really? Now, how can I go home without seeing that," I replied. "You've whetted my appetite. So, yes, I will stay another night if you are certain that's OK?"

"Only if you promise to sleep in a bed. You can't go hiking to the river without a proper night's sleep."

"Would you mind if Bailey shared my room?"

"Not at all," Bill replied.

I wanted to know more – about the area, the waterfall and about Bill. Why did he live in seclusion? That puzzled me. He had a caring manner and he was the type of man that you felt able to trust. When he spoke he looked at you, and when you were deep in conversation, he listened, really listened. It was almost as if you had met someplace before and were picking up where you left off.

When I came downstairs after changing, Bill had already prepared a casserole. After placing it in the oven, he asked me to keep an eye on it. "And if you put the dumplings in half an hour before we need to eat, about one o'clock, I'd be grateful. Then, I can get on with my other tasks," he said.

We shared a pot of tea and then Bill went out to make a start on the chicken run. After washing up, I went out to join him. We chatted effortlessly. Although I'm not at all practical, I passed him tools when requested and made sure he had a regular supply of coffee. Being outside made such a change. After spending time cooped up in my rented home, and prior to that an office environment, apart from when I travelled to various assignments, the fresh air blew the cobwebs away. As for Bill, the outdoor life was his passion. Birds and beasts, flowers and plants, he loved them all. On a practical level he looked as if he could turn his hand to anything. In fact, it surprised me a little he had let things go somewhat in his house. Perhaps, it needed a woman's touch!

Up against the shed I spied a small terracotta pot, which held a beautiful winter aconite. I took it inside. With its bright yellow blooms it made a lovely focus in the middle of the kitchen table. The small addition made the room look welcoming and sunny. I felt really content for some reason as I busied myself setting the table. Then, after popping the dumplings in, I had time to freshen up, before Bill came to check on lunch.

"Dumplings?" he asked.

"Yes, they're in. Be five minutes," I said cheerily.

Bill gave me the thumbs up! "So, you are not a bad cook then?" he said, with a wink. "Casserole smells delicious. Good team work I'd say."

"Well, it took a bit of effort," I replied.

After a nourishing lunch, we sat and drank our mugs of coffee over by the fire. Bailey sat close to

Bill, demanding to be stroked and petted, looking up at him with doleful eyes. My company and that of Bailey certainly seemed appreciated.

During the afternoon, Bill did odd tasks while I sat on the veranda, cossetted in warm blankets, attempting to get stuck into a recently published book I had wanted to read. However, I spent far more time admiring the view. As I watched this muscular man digging over his vegetable plot and tending to his chickens, I saw someone I liked. For a strong man he was very careful and gentle in his care. Even a worm stranded on a paving slab got lifted up carefully and placed on freshly dug soil. I admired Bill's tenderness and found myself foolishly daydreaming about his strong arms around me and how that might feel.

As dusk settled into night we went inside where we ate homemade crumpets, cooked on the hob and then toasted on the fire. Dripping with butter and treacle they made a delicious treat. After such a hearty lunch we needed nothing more. By nine o'clock, I was ready for an early night. All the fresh air had stilled my troubled mind and I hoped to get a good night's sleep.

The next morning I was wonderfully rested. I heard Bill downstairs talking to Bailey in a soothing, gentle voice, saying it was time his Mum was up! When I entered the kitchen the two of them were having a playful wrestle on the floor. Bill stood up as soon as he saw me and brushed himself down. He greeted me with a warm-hearted smile. I noticed he had trimmed his beard and even his stray, bushy eyebrows had been tamed. In fact, he looked particularly damn handsome in a rugged way. '*Stop right now, Abbie*,' I said to myself in warning.

Bailey came to greet me and then went back to eating his breakfast before chasing the empty bowl across the tiled floor.

"Sorry, he couldn't wait for you to get up Abbie," said Bill.

"Bet he drove you crazy until you gave in. But, he's a typical male, once he's fed and watered, he'll just ignore you!"

To prove me wrong, Bailey walked over to Bill wagging his tail and bowing in pursuit of more play. Bill laughed and told Bailey we needed to eat too.

"It's a fair walk to the waterfalls Abbie. You will need some energy," he said.

Breakfast, an omelette with grilled tomatoes, mushrooms and hunks of bread to mop up the juices tasted delicious. The fare could easily have competed with some B & B's I had stayed in. Bill was spoiling me.

"I like people who eat," chuckled Bill. "Though to look at you, don't suppose you've eaten like this for some time. You've not got a lot of meat on those bones."

"Um, I've not had much of an appetite of late. But, I have to say, even the rabbit stew you cooked up, with *my* help, was so flavoursome, despite my reluctance to try it."

"A lot of my ingredients come from the woods, fields and river nearby. Fresh, free range. As luck would have it, I've not been caught poaching, yet!" he chuckled.

"Bill! I thought you were a gentleman, someone who would stay on the right side of the law. Though, the free range fact is important to me too."

"I *was* the law," Bill replied. "For twenty years, man and boy, I did my service. But, one day everything changed." Then he coughed and hurriedly pushed his chair away from the table and dumped his plate and cutlery in the sink.

"So, I'm staying with an ex-copper then? Well, that makes me feel safer, I suppose. What made you leave?"

Bill ignored me. He didn't bother to turn round.

"Ten minutes? You'll be ready then?" he asked. "Be best to go and locate your car first and get it back here."

Nodding, I quickly swallowed the rest of my tea, wondering about Bill's reluctance to answer my question. No doubt he had a reason. Whatever it was, it wasn't my business to pry. After all we barely knew one another.

"Have you any idea where you left your car?"

"Sort of!"

"You came up from the road and over two fields? Did you see the lights of my cottage from there?"

"Yes. A beacon shining out through the darkness! But, seriously, Bailey will remember."

Sure enough, head down, sniffing and snorting, Bailey showed us the way. Bill, ever the prepared one, humped a can of petrol over the fields, just in case!

"I'm not that stupid," I told him.

Bill looked at me with a raised eyebrow. "Well, we'll see, won't we?" he replied, playfully nudging my arm.

Guess what? My car had indeed run out of fuel. Fortunately, Bill thought it amusing. He told me lumps of metal usually get you where you want to go if they have fuel in their tank.

"Lump of metal! Do you mind? She's called Betsey!" I replied, "a classic. And, just think, we would never have met if I hadn't broken down!"

"That's true. I will give you that," he said trying to sound serious, "then, that rabbit would have done me all week!"

Driving back towards The Hideaway seemed like heading home. Two days, and I was already in love with the place. My heart sank. Soon, I would need to leave this all behind.

Chapter 4

Before our walk to the falls, Bill suggested I change into something suitable to keep the chill at bay. Never one to be fashionable, I accepted the offer of some warmer items from his wardrobe. A brushed cotton shirt and an Aran sweater looked just the job. Though miles too big for me, I was happy with my choice of ill-fitting clothes. Practicality won over style. My reflection in the dressing table mirror, my knitted hat pulled down over my ears, showed someone set to go rambling.

"I'm sorted, shall we go?" I called out as I walked downstairs. With that Bailey came to my side in an instant, barking with excitement.

"You look a true explorer Miss Abigail! I will just grab my camera too, and then I'm ready. We are probably going to get a bit mucky, but the reward of some breathtaking views will make up for it, I promise."

When we arrived at the start of the circular walk, Bill told me tales about the Gubbins who lived in caves deep down in the rocky cliffs. The gang of outlaws, renowned for sheep stealing and being very unpleasant to anyone who ventured their way, lived back in the 16th century. "So, you have no reason to be fearful today," Bill added.

"That's good then! Even with your tales to try and scare me, making out parts of Dartmoor are bleak and foreboding, I'm sure this walk will be extraordinarily beautiful."

"It will. I'm just throwing a bit of history and mystery into the mix, that's all."

We arrived at the top of the gorge for the start of our walk into hidden depths. At first, I sauntered along without a care in the world, immersed in the amazing scenery. But, as the terrain grew more taxing, I realised I wasn't as fit as I thought.

"Sorry, for holding you up," I panted.

"It's not a race. I can keep to your pace so don't worry. If we rush we might miss something."

"Well, it's just as well we ate a hearty breakfast. You were right about needing some energy," I replied, wiping the sweat from my brow. In spite of the gentle breeze, I was cooking!

I unfastened my coat. Meanwhile, Bailey had energy enough for us both, pulling on his lead and carrying his bushy tail upright with all the excitement of this new environment with lots of different scents. I loved to see him enjoying himself.

The area consisted of ancient oak and hazel woods. Bill told me about the wildlife that lived there. He said we might be lucky and catch a glimpse of a dipper or an otter in one of the pools. All around us was a veritable feast for the senses and it was wonderful to be in the midst of such peace and tranquility.

As we walked on, the path became slippery, strewn with stones and pieces of slate. At one stage I almost lost my footing.

"Steady on," Bill said, quickly grabbing my arm and pulling me to safety. "I think you need to stay on the outside, away from the river now, even if it means you are up for sale!"

"That's what Dad used to say to my Mum. I've never heard anyone else ever use that particular phrase. I always wondered where the saying came from…"

"The good ol' days…. when women were ladies and men were gentlemen. A man always offered his left arm to his lady so his right hand was free to draw his sword if he needed to. Later on, having your lady on the inside gave her protection when carts drove by. Looking at the state of your clothes when I first saw you, it might have helped if I'd been close when you made your way up and over the fields!"

Bill chuckled, our eyes met and I saw warmth and caring. My heart lurched, attempting to tell me something. Everything around me seemed brighter and I felt so alive.

"Best get a move on," Bill insisted, interrupting the moment, "or darkness will descend and we might get lost. What's the time, anyway?"

Pushing my sleeve up I checked my watch and grinned. "Well, Bill, you will be very pleased to know, considering you tend to rely on maps and compasses, we are heading ESE."

Looking puzzled he replied, "I asked you the time!"

"Thing is, I seem to have put my watch on upside down and the digital reading shows ESE which means it's 3:53pm," I replied, light-heartedly.

Bill shook his head and chortled. The corners of his twinkling, hazel eyes crinkled when he laughed. I also noticed how the swelling on his forehead had changed from red to a bluish purple. Bless him. I wanted to kiss it better.

Bill broke into my daydream, "Come on, step on it Abbie, or we'll be caught out. Then, who knows, the Gubbins might appear and ensnare us."

Shivering, I pulled my hat down and buttoned my coat, telling Bill to stop scaring me. With my imagination taking control at the best of times, I didn't need it conjuring up weird, unforgettable stuff of nightmares. Bill's apology sounded genuine.

We carried on with our ramble, past trees with their gnarled bark begging to be stroked, their huge trunks longing to be hugged. The quiet rustle of leaves underfoot, the fresh air and the sound of running water provided a treasure worth enjoying. The whole area was a natural haven for wildlife. My senses drank it in. Lush green ferns thrived in sheltered shady positions and wild garlic, their dainty florets swaying above broad pointed leaves, provided a heady aroma. Bill, a habitual forager, said he often used the leaves as an alternative to spinach; it had a delicate taste. He also made wild garlic butter to enrich homemade broad bean hummus. He explained the leaves could be confused with those of lily of the valley, which is toxic, but if you simply crushed a leaf in the palm of your hand and then inhaled, you couldn't make a mistake. I tried it; he was right! There was no mistaking its pungency. The rich aroma made up a menu in my mind of steak and chips, a long forgotten meal. I hadn't ordered steak for years.

We plodded along and chatted freely, excitement building as the sound of the river increased in intensity. We talked about our love of photography and the way a moment gets captured for all time in a single shot.

"Pity that shot is often so hard to come by," Bill said. "I remember sitting by the side of the river for hours, trying to blend in with my surroundings, hoping to get a close-up of a kingfisher with a fish in its beak. Yes, I saw kingfishers and I saw fish, but not both at the same time. One day. I remain optimistic. It's a challenge, but I might get lucky."

"Wildlife can't be tamed, that's some of the problem. Like you, I find it a challenge. Readers look at a glossy picture in a magazine, but they have no idea that picture was one out of perhaps five hundred shots I took that day. Practice doesn't always make perfect, does it?"

"No, but what a buzz when it works!"

"Well, I don't know about you Bill, but I feel anticipation in the air. Either that or it's a shower on the way."

"Hope not, underfoot it's treacherous as it is."

Today's excursion was physically more challenging than my walk over the fields to find Bill's cottage. That was demanding in other ways because I didn't know where I was heading or what I'd find at the end. With Bill, difficulties appeared less troublesome. He looked out for me, especially when the terrain became more precarious as the path narrowed and the granite pathway became broodily dark. Then, when I reached out to hold his hand, he didn't pull away.

Steep steps took us further into the gorge where mist created an almost rainforest environment. Various types of ferns grew in abundance and lichen clung to rocks and trees. Spongy, green clumps of moss sparkled with dewy droplets of water, which seeped continuously down the rock face. My imagination saw us entering a prehistoric age. It was awesome. With all the recent rain the river pounded through the gorge, alerting us to the strength and magnificence of nature. As soon as we reached the waterfall itself, a stunning almost vertical drop down slippery bare rock, we both reached for our cameras, hoping to capture the beautiful sight. The cascade of water did indeed look like a bride's flowing gown.

"I see why it's a popular photo stop. So, yes, let's start focusing!"

"Come on then, strike a pose," Bill replied.

"If I must," I said, standing with one hand on my hip.

Bill smiled as he pointed his camera towards me. "That's good. Now half turn and look at the water. That's good."

I looked down and suddenly everything started to swim in front of my eyes. My arms flailed in the air as I desperately fought to stop myself from falling. Bill gasped, grabbed me and held me tight.

"Phew! That was close," he said. "Yes, a bit too close for my liking. Let's go home, shall we? Perhaps you can come again to see the rest."

I nodded in agreement as my heart settled.

On the way back to the cottage, Bill gave me all the background on the White Lady Falls, informing me that Gilpin had written about them after his visit in the early 1800s.

"To be honest, Gilpin wasn't impressed. He described seeing a spout rather than a cascade."

"Well, I was stunned, Bill. Can't wait to tell my brother and Aunt Bella about my whole adventure. I'm so glad I came."

"So, am I," said Bill, quietly.

Back at the cottage, Bill told me about Rachel Evans, a poet who had visited the falls in 1846.

"She wrote a marvellous poem. It begins, *we heard the rumbling waterfall…*"

He then proceeded to recite the whole poem, stanza by stanza. I didn't interrupt, once.

"Wow, you certainly had my attention there. What a memory, I must say. So you love poetry?"

"Yes. I have a copy of that poem somewhere. I love words, rhythm and rhyme. What about you Abbie?"

"Well, I love books, fiction, fact, poetry, Shakespeare too. Projects in my former employment included writing articles for publication. But, poems and stories I've penned myself, I've never shown them to anyone."

"You should. It might become more than a hobby."

"If only," I sighed. "But, when I say, I have never shown anyone, that's not quite true. I did share a special, personal story with someone, but he dismissed it straightaway. They were my innermost thoughts, my deepest feelings. I thought after reading it that he might realise how a certain situation had affected me. Really, I should have realized then…"

Remembering the occasion made me sad. I swallowed hard, trying to stop myself from weeping. But, Bill could tell I was upset and after hesitating briefly, wrapped his strong arms around me. I sobbed into his chest. He handed me his handkerchief. After drying my eyes I gave it back, flushed with embarrassment. The time wasn't right to unload all my secrets.

That evening we sat either side of a roaring log fire, sipping mulled wine. Although it wasn't Christmas, the cottage had a seasonal atmosphere about it. As candles glowed and soothing music played in the background, we toasted bread and spread it with butter and homemade blackberry jam; a perfect end to an almost perfect day. I looked across at Bill. I liked what I saw. Again, I started to weep, but for a different reason this time.

"I think I've caught a cold," I said, tearfully, blowing my nose. Though, I suspected it was more than a cold causing my tummy to dance and my eyes to water.

Chapter 5

Perhaps I had caught a chill after all. The night seemed freezing. I curled up into a ball to try and keep warm. I still couldn't sleep. My head was full of real and imaginary stories and questions about my new friend. Then there was Mike. Was my relationship with him truly over? I tossed and turned fitfully until the early hours, trying to find answers. It was well past three o'clock before my eyelids closed.

In the morning, a light knock on the bedroom door woke me. Bill brought me breakfast in bed. I readily took a sip of tea as he drew back the curtains.

"Surprise!" he said, pointing outside. Edging myself up on one elbow, I peered over to the window. It was snowing.

"I don't think you will be going anywhere today Abbie. The temperature really dropped overnight. And, there's something I need to show you. You see, I developed some of my photos, intending to give them to you as a souvenir, but..."

Bill sat down on the corner of the bed. "Look at this photo of the pool and the caves," he said calmly.

"What is that?" I asked, aghast.

"A Gubbin!"

"No! A Gubbin?"

"Not just any Gubbin. I'd swear its Richard Rowle, the King of the Gubbins. Have you read Westwood Ho? Charles Kingsley described the fear that moorland travellers had for the Gubbins, soldiers too. They never quartered in the area where the Gubbins lived. Seen to be above the law, the Gubbin clan apparently ceased to exist by the middle of the 17th century. Now, I wonder."

"Are you kidding? Is that supposed to be Richard Rowle standing in front of the caves where we walked yesterday?" I asked, peering closely at the photo.

"I think so."

I shook my head, puzzled. Ghosts, myths, legends; was this evidence? I had no way of knowing. But, how did the image appear? For I was looking at a perfect shot of a man clad in rags. He had filthy, straggly hair and narrowed eyes that showed no mercy. Was this a man who robbed and lived in caves where barefoot children ran and played in the dirt, described in literature as both a black-hearted villain and the Robin Hood of Dartmoor?

"But, that's not all. This one shows clearly the White Lady!"

Bill handed me another photo to scrutinize.

I looked and took a sharp intake of breath. Bill told me the photo was the one he took just before I stumbled and almost fell in the river.

"They say Abbie, that the White Lady appears when someone is in danger of drowning and saves them."

"You have that serious look. You really believe it, don't you?"

"Yes," Bill, answered calmly.

A chill ran through me. Staring, wide-eyed, I peered more closely at the shot. The white lady in the photograph was holding up her arms, almost welcoming my fall. I shivered.

"Don't worry Abbie, it's probably an illusion."

"Like my life; an illusion!" I said, laughing nervously. "Anyway, now I think it's about time I left, don't you?"

"If you must, but please don't worry. There must be some explanation. Let's forget about it. So, when does your new job start?"

"I don't have a new job. In fact, I've only just started sending out applications, although none of the jobs advertised really tempts me."

"Then stay. Please, one more day, Abbie. I don't want you leaving here worried or driving in this weather."

All the talk about Gubbins and the White Lady falls proved strangely intoxicating. Like a fairground ride it made me both scared and excited. I needed to know more. How was I supposed to get back to an ordinary life, find a job and a long-term home with all this in the back of my mind? Plus, Bill. Only, he wouldn't be in the back of my mind. I had turned a page of a book, had a glimpse of a chapter and a plot, but as yet I was unsure about the outcome or, whether I actually wanted to read the complete story. But, the character at the center of that story was Bill. He determined how it would end. One more day might make things clearer.

My decision delighted Bill but it also meant I had to call my brother, to tell him about my change of plan. Goodness knows what he might say. Still, it had to be done and so I asked Bill if we could go to the local village for me to make a call.

"Why didn't you say Abbie? I've got an old mobile. I keep it charged for emergencies but I've never used it. You can call with that if you like?"

"Never used it! How do you manage?" I asked.

"You've seen how I manage. Adequately, thank you Miss!"

Aiden kept repeating, "Staying with a man you just met? Someone you don't know?"

But, following a lengthy discussion, Aiden seemed to understand. Bill talked to him too, promising to see me off by the end of the week.

Bill thought I was lucky having Aiden, someone who cared about me so much. He told me no one would be troubled if he were alive or dead."

"Oh Bill. Don't say that. It's not true," I murmured.

"My own fault. See, I cut myself off from the outside world and any friends, years ago."

"Why?" I asked.

Bill shrugged his shoulders. For me the mystery deepened.

"Anyway, no more talk, let's have some action. We ought to go to the village and get some basic supplies, in case the snow gets worse. I mean, I can't believe how heavy it was during the night; a right blizzard."

"Well, let's hope that's it! If I end up staying any longer my brother will think I've been kidnapped!"

Bill's old four-wheeled drive coped readily with the terrain. Being chauffeured made a change. It gave me all the delights of going on an adventure without the danger of getting lost.

The small village itself was picture perfect with about twenty or so houses, two pubs and one little shop. With the snowy backdrop, it looked charming. Squeals of laughter greeted us, with children running amok throwing snowballs. One little boy dragged his teddy round on a handmade sled, stopping beside a snowman with its twiggy arms held aloft, red mittens waving a welcome. Bailey's head moved excitedly from side to side, eager to get involved, looking pretty silly with his pink tongue lolling out of the side of his mouth.

Bill turned to lock the car and a hastily thrown snowball hit him squarely on the shoulder.

"Sorry, Mister," called one of the children.

Laughing, Bill dusted himself down before throwing a softly aimed snowball back. Bailey tugged on his lead, keen to play. The children rushed to meet him as he lolloped towards them through the snow. He pirouetted with an open mouth, ready to catch snowballs as they threw them up in the air. Naturally, the snowballs turned to mush the minute he bit into them. The children giggled and Bailey ran from one to the other, ready for more, making lots of exaggerated movements, bowing in front of them, and wiggling his butt! We happily joined in with all the fun.

"Shall we make a snowman when we get back to the cottage and have hot chocolate and marshmallows," I said excitedly, caught up in the moment.

"Anything you want, Princess," Bill replied.

Princess? Well, all at once this down-trodden woman felt youthful and alive. Yes, the next chapter in *my* book had started to look quite promising!

We headed for the shop with a gaggle of children waving goodbye. It was so lovely; somewhere I could live, somewhere where time moved very slowly, gently, and somewhere where you strolled hand in hand with a loved one. *'Girlfriend, you are doing the romance bit again'* my inner voice whispered.

"Penny for them," said Bill.

"Just taking in the beautiful scene," I replied, hastily letting go of his hand.

"I don't bite you know! And, you grabbed *my* hand Abbie, without as much as by your leave!"

Blushing, I quickened my pace as I headed towards the gate of the whitewashed shop, which appeared to be the front room of someone's house. When I entered, it seemed as if I had stepped back in time, jolted back to childhood. My grandmother ran a village store in her front room.

Grannie's shop sold bunches of bright, golden chrysanthemums in late summer, which she grew in her back garden and produce from farms; eggs, cabbages, carrots and fresh new potatoes, all locally sourced. I remembered picking juicy, red plums and bright green cooking apples in season and putting them out for display in large wooden crates outside the shop window. Jars of homemade pickles and jams, honey, lavender soaps and freshly baked bread, Grannie's cakes and pastries, they all delighted her loyal customers.

Smiling, I thought of the haberdashery section. One of my tasks was packing new supplies into boxes and tins stacked haphazardly on a table. Ribbons and buttons required coordinating and cards of hooks and eyes and bra fasteners needed arranging. The table had a cloth draped over it, which reached to the floor.

It was a great hiding place. Concealed behind the tablecloth, with a jar of pickled onions that I'd managed to smuggle to the back of the shop, I used to feel wickedly grown-up. I'd prise off the lid, trusting the satisfying pop wouldn't find me out. I licked my lips and squeezed my eyes shut, recalling the sharp, vinegary taste.

Bill purchased some basics, tea and flour, plus a truckle of Curworthy chipple cheese. He told me the cheese was made on a farm in the shadow of Dartmoor.

"Should go well with that rye seeded loaf I made, before you were up, with some tomatoes and homemade pickles."

I nodded in agreement.

"As for dinner, that will be the rest of the rabbit beneath a short crust pastry topping. If in doubt, the scales will show you've enjoyed your little break!"

"But, I have."

"Hey, do you fancy a drink? You're not in a hurry, are you?"

"Yes, and no! That would be lovely."

"I know a great little pub by the river."

"Sounds perfect."

I mean I had all the time in the world. I didn't need to be anywhere else today, or tomorrow, or any other day for that matter. That's what my heart was telling me even though my head screamed, job applications, work, and a new home.

The pub, a larger version of Bill's cottage had low, dark oak beams, a huge inglenook and lime washed walls. We sat over by the window looking down towards the river; a babbling flow of clear, crystal water, rippling over moss covered rocks. Bailey lay under the table on the floor enjoying the coolness of the flagstones. Totally relaxed, I drank in the scenery. Suddenly, a kingfisher, a shiny iridescent blue dived like a dart into the water. It surfaced with a small fish, taking it to a snow dusted perch on the bank.

"See what I mean Bill? You need patience, time and a camera, everywhere you go."

Bill smiled. "You are so right. Well, perhaps we can come again, with a camera in tow. Might have to leave Bailey at home though."

Home? Yes, Bill's cottage felt like home. Was it too soon to mention how I felt?

Bill interrupted my thoughts. "You might not have got your perfect photo shoot, but I hope you enjoyed the day?" he said.

"Immensely."

"Cheers, good health."

"Cheers," I replied, absentmindedly.

"So, is there anything or anywhere you would like to see before you leave Abbie?"

I looked at Bill's muscular arms as he pushed the sleeves of his sweater up. His hands, strong hands, looked so unlike Mike's, which were soft and smooth and hadn't done a day's labour in their life. Yet, they did make me swoon when he caressed and stroked my back so soothingly. Now, I wondered what Bill's hands would feel like, gently caressing my breast.

'*Enough*,' my inner voice screamed. Yes, enough. He would probably take one look at my body and then leap away, disgusted.

"Abbie, Abbie!"

"Oh sorry, I was miles away."

"Take me with you! It looked like you were in a special place."

I blushed. "Actually, I don't think you would like to be there. But, shall we go now, back to yours?"

At the cottage we shared a ploughman's lunch in front of a roaring fire; the relaxed style was something I could easily get used to. Bailey sat close by, hoovering up any crumbs that fell on the floor. (He had no shame or manners.) Bill opened the bottle of Pebblebed Red that I'd bought in the village shop. A local wine, described as 'ideal for enjoying in good company,' was exactly that. A deep, red ruby colour, fruity and light, we shared the whole bottle between us. It helped loosen our tongues and made conversation between us very easy.

Bill looked very comfortable sitting with his head resting back on the chair, his eyes closed. The cut on his forehead had almost healed and the swelling had subsided too. The bruise though still evident had turned from red to bluish-purple. When it faded to yellow, I knew I'd be far away.

"Does your head still hurt?" I asked, tactfully, thinking if he said it hurt like hell, then I could offer to stay on a few more days.

"No, not at all. I was lucky," Bill said, blinking.

"Be more careful in the future, won't you?"

"I will certainly try. The next stranger that darkens my door might not be as friendly!"

Bill then asked what brought me back to England as I had already said how much I loved the States and the life I lived there. Sparing some finer details, I told him I'd lost my job. Mentioning it brought back sadness.

"It was my dream job. Then, *he* fired me," I blurted. "He never even bothered with a decent explanation. That really hurt." I started to cry and turned away.

"Oh Abbie, sometimes no amount of explaining situations changes them. Life isn't always fair, is it?" Bill said, reaching across and gently touching me on the shoulder. His sympathy only made me cry more.

"I'm sure he's not worth it."

"No, he isn't! He really isn't," I replied. "I honestly thought he cared. Obviously I have little sense when it comes to relationships."

"Sounds like he wasn't the one for you. One day I'm sure Mr. Right will drop into your life and sweep you off your feet. Then, whatshisname will seem like a bad dream, best forgotten."

I wiped my tears with the corner of my sleeve. Bill reached across and patted my hand. I pulled away as if I'd been stung.

"Sorry, I was still thinking of Mike."

"Mike? You mean, him?"

"Yes, my old Boss; old boyfriend too."

"Right. Old fool as well?"

I smiled weakly. "Perhaps."

I felt drained. It was time to change the subject. "Well, after my little display perhaps it's time you told me a little about yourself?"

"What would you like to know? It's been some time since I talked about myself," he said.

"Oh, I don't know really. How about you tell me what brought you here for a start."

"Start, that's a good word to use."

Bill coughed. "I'm warning you though. Like your story, we are not talking about happily ever after."

"Please, don't tell me if it's upsetting."

"You are a good listener Abbie. This might be therapeutic."

Bill looked down, took a deep breath and began.

"It's not that I wanted to obliterate the past, but it was necessary to have a new beginning. Somehow, somewhere, I needed to find an inner peace. As I mentioned before, I was in the Police force."

It surprised me to learn that Bill had been married. He hadn't mentioned that before. Still, why would he? We were only just getting to know one another and I was sure there would be other secrets and stories to be told if our relationship deepened. Bill then explained that he had met his wife during his time in the force. Half-heartedly, he tried to joke about them being seen as partners in crime. I smiled and nodded in encouragement as I could tell he was finding it difficult going back over his previous life.

"After we married, Alice made a decision. She would resign from the force when we had children. Being in the murder squad meant long hours plus, it was emotionally draining. Alice wasn't cut out to be desk bound, that wasn't what her career had been about. With an aptitude and keenness for gardening and the love of the outdoors, she hoped to retrain and become a landscape gardener. Yes, down to the last detail, she thought it out, describing how a potential little Billy or baby Alice would be content to watch their mummy at work. Oh, we both had so many plans … so many…" With that, Bill shook his head and covered his eyes.

"Please, if it's painful, don't say any more," I said, holding his hand. "There will be another time."

"I don't know. I'm not sure there will be."

What was he telling me? Once I left that was it? Why did men always back away from me?

My eyes filled with tears. Bill thought my crying was in sympathy and began to tell me more, albeit hesitantly.

They had both been on duty one fateful night. An urgent call saw them dispatched separately to a back street address. The caller, frantically screaming, informed the police, her ex-boyfriend had a gun and he was trying to get into her house.

Blue lights flashing, they arrived with backup outside the address. All was quiet. Curtains tweaked across the street, but there was no sign of a disturbance. A neighbour said they had not heard anything amiss. Armed officers approached the house from the front where Bill took up his position. Other armed officers and Alice, went to the rear of the terrace. There was no sign of anything untoward. A call was put through to the person inside. She told them it was all a mistake; there was nothing wrong. She was lying.

"Within minutes, the situation changed. To cut a long story short, a hostage situation developed and went on for two hours until, the man finally let his former girlfriend leave the house. Shaken, but physically uninjured, an ambulance took her to hospital. After negotiations, the boyfriend finally gave himself up. He was arrested. That seemed to be the end of what had been a stressful shift. By the time it was over, Alice and I were both due to be off duty but we still needed to write up our reports."

Bill was stuttering a little now; finding it difficult to speak. I told him he didn't have to tell me more.

"When we were done, we left the station together. We talked of getting a takeaway on the way home. We were shattered, it was dark, and the roads were wet. Then, from out of nowhere, a car driven at high speed lunged out of a side street straight into our path. I didn't have chance to avoid it. Abbie, it was terrible, the dreadful noise and then this overpowering silence."

Bill wept. Shocked, I didn't know what to say. After a few moments, Bill got up from his chair and reached for the photo on the mantelpiece.

"This is Alice; my dear Alice. I couldn't save her. I couldn't save her." Bill traced his index finger down the front of the photo before placing it back above the fireplace.

"The impact crushed the passenger side of the car. Alice took the full force and she died at the scene. Guilt, the sense of helplessness almost killed me too. That's why I had to get away and why I needed to leave the force and have this new beginning. No one could convince me otherwise. Here, I can be me and not, you know, the cop who lost his wife. After I resigned, I didn't wish to see old mates on a social basis either. The reminder was too great, too heartbreaking. I could only take so much."

"I think I understand," I mumbled quietly.

"Eventually, I came across The Hideaway, which was up for sale. I didn't hesitate. It offered the escapism I was searching for."

"So, how long have you lived here?"

"Seven years, thereabouts. My life, my journey here wasn't easy, now this is my home and I'm living. Yes, somewhat simply I'd have to agree."

"After all you've been through, I can see how living here provides you with everything you need."

"Almost everything. But, Alice would be nudging me, telling me to get on with my life. She lost hers and wouldn't want me to waste mine. I need to give her that respect, when I'm ready."

My heart broke for him. There in front of me, sat this big brave man looking like a small boy who needed a cuddle. I wanted to get up and put my arms around him, but I was scared. Bill's vulnerability was unnerving in some way. Until now I had only seen his strength. I wept, feeling his pain.

"Abbie, I'm so sorry. I didn't want to upset you," he said, wiping his eyes with the back of his hand as he offered me his hankie.

I reached across to take it. Our fingers touched, we looked at one another and attempted to smile. Then, the next moment we were holding one another close, giving comfort. We both knew that one day we might be able to compartmentalize our happier memories, keeping them safe in our hearts. Now, both good and bad memories were still surface deep; a slight scratch and they easily came flooding back.

At some point, I hoped Bill would allow me to be part of a new friendship circle, when he felt ready to make one. In fact, I longed to be at the center as it radiated out, giving Bill the happiness he deserved.

"So, will you visit this area again?"

"Depends. If I get invited!" I replied, smiling awkwardly.

Chapter 6

I called Bailey. He rushed into the living room with his new toy; one of Bill's old socks, with a tennis ball in the foot. He looked quite dangerous, swinging it around, banging it haphazardly against the furniture.

"Want to take your toy with you boy?" Bill asked, bending down to ruffle his coat. With exuberance Bailey leapt up, swiping the sock towards Bill's head.

"Steady on old fella. I don't want another knock on the head or your Mum might have to stay and look after me!" Bill exclaimed, putting his hands up in defense.

I knew it was only banter, but, oh, how I wished Bailey would catch Bill good and proper so I had a valid excuse to stay.

Leaving was emotional. We had only spent a couple of days together, but we seemed to get on famously during that time, after our somewhat uneasy start. As for Bailey, he had made a new, dear friend.

"Well, this is it then, I suppose."

"Take care," Bill replied. "Write if you can, visit if you must, but don't worry about giving me any warning about when to expect you. Come any time – some time soon, perhaps."

I nodded, unable to speak. Bill followed me out to my car, hugged Bailey goodbye, before settling him down in the back seat. Then he kissed my cheek. I looked into his beautiful eyes one more time. As I climbed into the driver's seat, we said our goodbyes, both trying to sound cheerful. Driving away from the cottage was difficult. I waved until Bill was out of sight. Sadly, he had sorted my satnav and so, I had no reason to land up back where I started. However, I could barely see the route on the screen through my veil of tears. Only, the vocal instructions were clear; still with an American accent.

By early evening, I reached Aiden's home. Full of concern he ran out to meet me.

"Whatever were you thinking of? Dad would be turning over in his grave, worrying about you."

"Restless, thinking I might have found *the one*!" I replied.

"Oh, Abbie! Well, tell me all. Stay tonight, then we can catch up properly."

"OK. But first, I need a long soak in the bath and a change of clothes, then I will answer all those questions you're dying to ask."

Aiden smiled, before walking off to make final preparations for our meal. I knew, whatever I told him, he'd probably think I'd gone mad. But, I was missing Bill already. Secretly, I hoped he was missing me too.

After my bath, I padded back to the spare bedroom. Large and luxurious with pretty bedding, it spoke of good taste. The colours blended with the distinctive pattern of the wallpaper that an interior designer friend of Aiden's had suggested. Everything coordinated beautifully and it looked lovely. I just preferred a bit of wear and tear to show that things had been used and loved. Bill's cottage suited my idea of a long-term home. Something like The Hideaway would suit me fine.

"At last. Did you fall asleep?" Aiden said, slamming the door of the Aga, before pouring us both a large glass of red wine. "Dinner will be about ten minutes."

"I had a little snooze, yes. What are we having? It smells wonderful."

"Just rustled up a lasagna, nothing special."

"Mum's recipe?"

"Of course."

"Then, it will taste delicious."

We sat next to each other behind a long table in the open plan kitchen area. Natural light flooded the room, which had allocated zones for cooking, dining and relaxing. Solid oak beams, high ceilings and granite stone floors gave the room an enormous sense of space. Sliding doors led out onto a patio and beyond that flowerbeds were full of topiary balls, evergreen ferns and hellebores in shades of dusky plum, creamy white and softest pink. Aiden had spent his inheritance wisely. He had built a home to be proud of. My share of the money was still tucked away in the bank. I simply did not know what to do with it.

Although Aiden's home was vast, it had a lovely atmosphere and was very welcoming. Under-floor heating made it warm and toasty. It just needed a couple of children running around, chasing one another, and a wife of course. But, Aiden hadn't met the right person to share his life with yet. Someone he would be content to spend the rest of his days loving and fussing over. And, to be honest, that was exactly what I wanted too. Yes, I was more than ready to settle down. On thinking this, an instantaneous picture of Bill came to the forefront of my mind. *'Please, don't do this,'* my inner voice screamed out.'

"Abbie, you are away with the fairies again."

"Sorry Aiden. Talking of fairies, wait till I tell you all about the Gubbins and the White Lady. You will think I've totally lost it!"

"Ok. Let me dish up, then fill me in."

After I've told him about my adventure, I waited for Aiden's response.

"I don't know what you want me to say. Perhaps Aunt Bella can talk some sense into you. She's coming tomorrow for a few days."

"Is she? How lovely. Mind you, I wonder what she's been up to lately. Every holiday she takes she meets someone! Remember last time? That chap, Malcolm Monroe? Now, he was odd!"

"Different, just different, I'd say. Anyway, after all your ramblings about myths and legends and your new friend, this might bring you back down to earth."

Aiden handed me an envelope. Even without looking at the sender's address, the American postage stamps told me straightaway who had mailed it. Holding my breath, I turned the envelope over in my hands, daring myself to open it. All sorts of thoughts tumbled through my mind. Was Mike missing me now? Was my old job up for grabs? Had Mike had a change of heart? I was heartbroken when we parted. Now, just touching the envelope, which Mike had handled, made me want to kiss it. Confused? My mind was totally scrambled.

"For goodness sake. Just open it and read it will you," ordered Aiden.

"Ok, ok Aiden. Stop rushing me."

Out of the envelope tumbled a card with a photo of Mike's father on the front. On the reverse was advice about his passing. His funeral, in a week's time would be held at The West Hill Funeral Home, Bala Cynwyd, followed by a gathering in the Atrium. Underneath the details was a short, handwritten note: *Be good to see you.* That's all it said. Someone had signed it on Mike's behalf.

I stared at the photograph and thought of Mike. Poor man, he must be distraught. Mike and his father had been so close. It was difficult to imagine Mike facing all this on his own.

"I don't know what to do," I told Aiden. "Mike will be lost without his father. I feel sad just thinking about how he will struggle."

"For goodness sake, Abbie. I suggest you concentrate on finding a job and forget about men. You can't help everyone, even in their hour of need!"

But, Aiden also suggested it wouldn't hurt if I sent Mike a condolence card. After all, Mike and I had been much more than acquaintances.

I stayed awake most of the night, tossing and turning, trying to sort out the best course of action. My mind swung like a pendulum, this way and that. When morning came, I had made my decision. Against Aiden's wishes, I booked a trip to Philadelphia – the City of Love.

"Give my love to Aunt Bella. Tell her sorry I missed her. As soon as I get back I will arrange a visit."

"That's if you come back," Aiden said moodily.

"Of course I will. And look after Bailey, please."

Throughout the flight my mind filled with a mixture of emotions. It seemed wrong to speak of the dead in a disparaging way, but since his father's death, perhaps Mike had finally earned the right to make his own decisions. Maybe the reason our relationship floundered no longer existed. Just yesterday, Bill had been at the forefront of my mind. Now, I wondered if my love affair with Mike was about to be rekindled! Why had I placed myself in the centre of such confusion? Common sense told me, I should have listened to Aiden, but when was I ever sensible?

At the Airport, Mike looked tall and lean and handsome as ever, even with the dark circles under his eyes. He kissed my cheek and politely thanked me for coming over.

"I expect you're tired," he said. "But I can take you straight to your Hotel and then you can unpack and get some rest."

"Oh, I thought you might want me to stay with you," I replied, as I linked my arm through his. "I'd like to help. There must be something I can do?"

Mike shrugged me off. When I looked up into his face, I saw tears. "Abbie, I'm so sorry. Not now. Forgive me. I need to sort this myself. You do understand?"

"Of course. I just hoped you might like me around."

"No, not now," he replied, flatly. "Like I said, I have so much to do – the funeral and all. In fact, be best if you do some sightseeing or meet up with your old friends in the City for the next day or two."

What old friends I wanted to ask. I hadn't kept in touch with anyone. Obviously Mike wasn't quite himself. After the funeral, there would be plenty of time to be together.

The hotel Mike booked me into was situated in one of the oldest neighbourhoods in Philadelphia, in the historic District itself. Cobbled streets were steps away from world-class restaurants and shopping. My room was huge with a bed of gigantic proportions. I had no reason at all to complain, apart from the fact I had no one to snuggle up to under the soft, silk sheets and comforter at bedtime. Not only was I alone in the City, I was lonely too.

The next day, I decided to go sightseeing, to keep myself busy. I had always wanted to visit the Dream Garden in Washington Square, in the lobby of the Curtis Centre, so I headed there first. The largest Tiffany piece in the world, a beautiful mural didn't disappoint. Made up of more than 100,000 pieces of favrile glass in 260 different colours, the brilliantly hued work deserved all its rave reviews.

Opposite the Curtis Centre, the Independence National Historic Park beckoned me in. I had been there many times before, but still found it interesting. I wandered round, taking photos of landmarks such as Independence Hall and the Liberty Bell. My day of sightseeing gave me the same feeling I had on looking closely at a favourite painting; no matter how often I viewed it, there was always something new to discover.

After a tiring day, I booked a table, for one, in the hotel Restaurant. On the menu, alongside other delicacies, they had Brussels sprouts as an appetizer! They didn't sound appetizing at all. Instead, I chose some olives and dipping bread as my starter together with a large glass of Pinot Grigio.

Sitting at a table on my own didn't trouble me. I wasn't up to making polite conversation with so much on my mind, trying to figure out why Mike was so detached. Why had he invited me over if he intended to ignore me? Perhaps the grief at losing his father had exposed him to untold stress and given time he would feel ready to explain. He had looked somewhat confused and anxious, even at the airport.

I called him when I got back to my room. Our conversation was pretty stilted, although, he said he'd like to meet up for lunch the following day. That night I hardly slept, wondering what we both might say. I needed clarity.

The following morning, Mike appeared whilst I was eating breakfast. That was a surprise. I was pleased. During my working life in America, I'd been informed that breakfast meetings developed close business relations, now I hoped that extended to personal relationships too. However, that notion was soon swept aside.

I told him about my excursions the day before, but Mike showed little interest. The death of his father appeared to have hit him really hard. He barely made any eye contact with me at all.

"Mike, is there something you need to tell me?" I suddenly blurted out.

He looked directly at me.

"I just never thought for one moment you would fly over," Mike said.

I smiled and reached across the table for his

hand. That's when I saw it, the ring.

"Mike, is that your father's ring?" I asked, unsure whether to sound solemn, serious or scared.

"No. I should have told you at the Airport…"

My tummy flipped over. I anticipated bad news.

"Why am I here?" I whispered.

"I don't know Abbie. Why? I never asked you to come."

I was flabbergasted. The news meant Mike never had any intention of picking up where we left off. Stupidly, I had completely misunderstood. Mike's longings and mine were completely different. This wasn't about me at all.

Mike pushed his chair away from the table and looked towards the door, smiling. I followed his gaze. Framed in the doorway, stood the reason I should have stayed away - a stunning, beautiful girl. I say girl, because she looked about twenty years old; long, blond, shiny hair and legs up to her armpits. Honestly, she had it all. My heart pounded so hard in my chest, I was sure everyone could see it.

Mike held out his hand out and she floated across. She looked up into his face and he kissed her, full on the lips. I simply wanted to die.

"Abbie, I was about to tell you. This is Vanessa."

"Hello Abbie," she purred. "I'm so glad I've gotten to meet you. I sent the card about Mr. Johnson, and I'm so pleased you could make it. I told Mike it was a good idea. It's so great to meet someone Mike used to know."

I was speechless. Vanessa had encapsulated the truth in one sentence because that's all I was – someone Mike *used* to know. The minute I saw that loving look in his eyes as he glimpsed Vanessa, I understood. She was the one. Someone he desired.

Our goodbyes were brief. I booked a return flight straightaway. Then, at the airport, while I waited to board, I did something I should have done ages ago. I deleted Mike's precious voice mails from my phone.

Chapter 7

The long flight home gave me plenty of time to think about my relationship with Mike, and question why I had fallen for him so readily in the first place. A glance, a few words and he had me captured. Was I desperate to be shown affection, to be loved, any man at that stage could win me round? Perhaps, I thought sadly.

When I was diagnosed with cancer, I was aware that in order to save my life, things needed to be done. A gentle approach wasn't required in dealing with this horrid disease. My surgery consisted of completely removing my left breast along with a sample of lymph nodes from under my arm. I was offered reconstruction too, but I couldn't face further, lengthy surgery. When they spoke of muscle flaps, growing tissue, even tattooing a nipple, I turned away.

My brother and Aunt Bella gave me lots of support at that time. Aunt Bella spoke in a positive way, reassuringly. She came with me when I got measured for my first proper prosthesis and took me for a celebration drink afterwards. Dear Aunt Bella, she knew how to lighten the atmosphere, toasting,

"To our new friend. May she always keep you balanced!"

In time, slipping the artificial breast into my bra became as ordinary as putting on my shoes. In fact I grew personally fond of it. Like an old friend, it offered comfort; it made me whole. And, when I stood naked in front of the mirror in my bedroom, I liked to gently press the palm of my hand over my scar, to feel my flesh pulsating softly with each heartbeat.

As the scar faded, my overwhelming thoughts about cancer, last thing at night and first thing each morning, gradually faded too. What took longer to improve was my confidence, especially around men. I used to think they looked directly at my breasts when talking to me, that they knew. Trouble was, I was almost desperate to be found attractive, womanly and sexy in spite of my loss. To be held in a loving embrace by a man who treated me with kindness and respect, someone who could love me in spite of everything. It had seemed a distant fantasy. Until, I met Mike.

Stupidly, as our relationship developed, I thought my dreams had come true. Mike was somewhat distant if his father was around, but his father had been his Boss. At work, he could hardly whisper sweet nothings in my ear. Back in my apartment, when there were just the two of us, he used to say that he loved me, over and over. Even so, I wondered if he was in love with the idea of love, as being intimate seemed awkward and embarrassing. He found my scars difficult to look at. Mike's solution came in the form of giving me gifts of expensive lingerie, exquisite, frothy and frilly, daintily embroidered, clothing to cover me up. He told me pretty underwear might help me feel more feminine! And, not once did he remove my bra or make love to me fully undressed. No, a part of me became secret, hidden, undisclosed. This made me sad and self-conscious but reluctantly I accepted Mike's way of dealing with my situation. Now, I wanted to focus on how I dealt with it all, instead of placing someone else in the equation. The answer lay in finding my own self-worth. Yes, I had losses in my life but Aunt Bella's always said; "Sometimes you need to lose something precious in order to gain something priceless."

Hampshire, a stunning county offered opportunities to concentrate on my photography once more. The New Forest had pastureland, heathland and wetland, wild ponies and deer. The sea too was within easy travelling distance, so I had the best of both worlds. Photographing yachts whilst travelling on the ferry to the Isle of Wight soon became a huge draw and one of my timeless past-times. The island itself gave me splendid sights and scenes to capture, pretty villages, castles, St Catherine's Oratory which looked like a rocket about to take off, Ventnor gardens, Carisbrooke Castle, Osborne House, the list of photographic opportunities was endless. Standing on top of the hill by the old rocket test station gave me great views of the beach far below and curving from the headland, the Needles, a glorious view. Once I began to see my albums filling up with such new, spectacular photographs, my heart and mind felt stilled.

Some say a house is not a home without a dog – well, I had Bailey. But, I decided it was high time I unpacked my boxes, to allow my house to look lived in. It needed some personal effects about to give it personality. I thought of Bill's cottage – it was homely, comfortable, warm and welcoming – oh, so warm and welcoming! But before I got side-tracked, I made a call to collect some of my boxes, currently held in storage.

Driving back to my rented house, my car packed to the gunnels, I looked forward to arranging some of my mementoes from various places and making the house look more like a home. Books on the bookcase, my favourite pictures on the wall, and photos about the place seemed far better than living with bare furniture and blank walls. Aiden had kept saying it looked like I was just passing through, that a Motel had greater atmosphere than where I lived.

Several boxes contained novels that meant something to me. Either they had been given to me as gifts or I had bought them and read them again and again. Often books captured my imagination and needed to be appreciated more than once. Nowadays, I knew the majority of people read from a screen but I still preferred to turn the page of a book instead of scrolling through. I also had dozens of photograph albums. Again, I wasn't one who stored everything on a mobile device. I was a page-turner.

However, once I started peeking through my collections, releasing memories, unpacking took far longer than it ought. For the whole afternoon, I delved into the past. Unlike my work portfolios, my albums contained photos from childhood. My lovely parents Davina and Jim, they looked so content and happy. There was a photo of me on my fifth birthday, holding a rag doll Mum had made. Mum was giggling and Dad was smiling while Aiden had his arm around me and was saying, 'cheese.' Both my parents died when I was in my early twenties, more than sixteen years ago. They had my brother and me quite late. Somehow Mum always seemed old, but so very young at heart. I think it was the fashion back then, permed hair, grey, never tinted, it added years. However, as they always looked the same, incongruously, in my eyes they never aged!

The album I put together in America showed many of my favourite haunts. Looking again at the scenery brought back some great memories. Overall, it had been an interesting experience. Now, I was ready to move on. Even so, I left the few photos of Mike in the book, as I didn't want to tear them out and spoil the pages! Peering at the photos I even managed a reluctant smile. Yes, he looked happy back then. Indeed for a time we were both happy. Honestly, it made little sense to dwell on anything other than the good times. I had done a lot of soul searching and had started to realise it was unhelpful to sit and dwell on things that were not in my capacity to solve. It was high time I concentrated on finding a job instead.

Freelance work offered greater freedom, more choice, a better work life balance so that seemed worth considering. Working at my own speed, the hours I wanted, taking breaks when I felt like it, I had missed that. Aunt Ella insisted life was about taking risks and doing what you wanted, not what someone else made you do. According to my Aunt you only know what you are looking for when you find it. She often went off on paths of exploration. Her latest letter highlighted the fact. It was a story in itself.

Dearest Abbie

I hope my latest adventure makes you think about having one of your own. You never know where it might lead! Anyway, this is what happened to me recently.

The forecast said, wintery showers but you know me; I'd trudge through any weather to discover more about our family history. I intended to follow up on my recent discoveries. Remember I told you about great Uncle Richard who set off for America to seek his fortune? Well, I was going back to see where he lived during his formative years…

When the red double decker approached the stand I read the destination – Garsington. Absentmindedly, I thought that's where I wanted to go. I mean Garsington and Cassington, they sound similar don't they? Anyway dear, I climbed aboard.

The bus was packed and so I quickly sat down near the front, alongside a well-upholstered lady wearing a bright red wool coat, black leather gloves and a smart, neat black hat, worn tilted to one side. She appeared about fortyish but the perfume she was drenched in had an old fashioned, highly fragranced, rose scent, which reminded me of my Mother, your Nannie Shaw. The perfume conjured up scenes of picnics by the river, the blanket spread out on the grass and me and your dad trying to catch minnows in empty jam jars; a time of pleasures and pursuits.

All that daydreaming ceased as the bus rattled out of the station and turned sharply into the main street. Then, I had to grab the handrail to stop myself falling sideways every time the bus lurched. Otherwise, I was in danger of either falling into the aisle or into the lap of the lady next to me. I don't know which would have been the most unpleasant! Fortunately, at the next stop, my well-padded neighbour got off. That gave me the opportunity to move across into the warmest of seats, next to the window.

More settled, I gazed out at the scenes passing by and smiled at my reflection. I was wearing my purple-rimmed glasses with my purple coat and the pair of dangly silver earrings you gave me for my birthday, the ones with little butterflies on them. Did I tell you, I've had pink highlights put through my hair? Goodness, might be a small tattoo next!

Anyway, back to my day out. Before long, I recognised the scenery passing by and wondered if the bus was heading in the right direction. But, I felt too embarrassed to get up and ask the driver if he's sure I'm on the correct bus. After all, when I showed him my bus pass and said the destination, he had nodded and smiled without a word. Mind you, the young blonde behind me could have distracted him. Of course Abbie, as you've probably guessed, when the bus reached Garsington, it's not where I wanted to be.

I asked the driver when was the next bus to Cassington was due. He peered at his watch and told me, "Bout, an hour love. Get yourself a cuppa I'd say, there's a storm on the way."

Well, I was hardly prepared. Yes, I can hear you saying, "You're not safe to be let out on your own!"

But, Abbie, the village looked pleasant enough, a church, a school and beautiful thatched Cotswold stone cottages, with gardens surrounded by dry stonewalls and neat grass verges. At least I hadn't been dropped off down some country lane in the dark! (Sorry dear, Aiden told me what happened to you recently!) Plus, a road sign by the war memorial showed I was only five miles from Oxford - familiar territory.

I wandered off and found the Three Horseshoes pub on the green. Like the man suggested, I wanted to get myself a cuppa – or glass of wine! The atmosphere inside was very welcoming with a log fire burning brightly that added to the cosy atmosphere. An original feature, a ships keel supporting the ceiling looked magnificent. As I walked towards the bar, the sense of yesteryears gathered in every nook and cranny of the building and I wondered what they would tell me if walls could speak.

"Yes? Can I help?" offered a tall lean young man, sporting a tidy beard, a roguish smile and a pair of tortoiseshell coloured spectacles.

I asked for a large glass of house red; good for the blood! I decided to take a look at the menu too. The barman was very friendly and told me to take a seat. I sat by this huge inglenook with its lovely smell of wood smoke. The fire crackled and little golden sparks darted out to smoulder on the hearth. It brought back wonderful memories from childhood, of visiting your great Nan and Grampy in their cottage for Sunday tea. Your dad loved crumpets toasted in front of the fire, or toast, which Grampy often ended up burning. He used to set to, scraping away at the scorched bits, sending burnt offerings all over the place.

When the barman came to my table he said, "Not many strangers arrive by bus; the village isn't really on the map as a day-trippers paradise. You see, we're funny folk, us locals!" Then he winked and grinned, as he set a glass of Merlot wine down on the polished oak table.

"Tell the truth – I wasn't heading this way when I got on the bus," I told him. "Took the wrong one! Still, now I'm here I might as well take a look around your beautiful village; after lunch."

"Just mind out for the Ghost of Garsington!" he warbled.

My eyes lit up. I was intrigued and asked him where the haunting took place. He told me that I would need to stay until nightfall so that made me decide to book in for the night to one of the rooms. I told him spontaneity was my middle name! That made him chuckle.

Course, I had no change of clothes or anything. Still it was only one night. And the room was delightful. The bed was very comfy with crisp cotton sheets, woollen blankets and a traditional Candlewick bedspread. I was happy because, as you know dear, duvets aren't really my thing. Anyway, with nothing to unpack, I was soon ready to set off for a good walk. I decided I needed the exercise to give me an appetite for my evening meal. So I wrapped up warmly for my stroll in the late afternoon light. I was glad I had my thermal vest on I can tell you, or the chill would have got to my bones. Only, the metal pub sign swaying and swinging mournfully above the pub door gave me a warning. Pub signs always do – I've always had this inherent odd feeling that one will come crashing down on me one day. My vivid imagination suggests that's how my previous life came to an end. Well, unless my end was even more sinister. Perhaps I was beheaded by guillotine! Unreasonable I know, but when have I been rational?

The air seemed to smell of a coming snow shower – an almost hand washed scent of freshness. The sky was grey and the clouds low. Birds huddled together on bare branches. I can see you now, shaking your head and saying, "Whatever next!" But, you know, after my forays I always return home unscathed, full of excitement, ready to explain what I've been up to.

On the edge of the village sat Garsington Manor. That's where they hold an Opera Season during the summer. I read about it recently. Although that's not my kind of entertainment there's a possibility that one day I might go. My Mother used to say, how could anyone possibly know what they like or loathe if they've never even tried it and there is a particular piece on the sound track of the film Philadelphia, La Mamma Morta from Madam Butterfly that I love so, that's a start! I expect you remember, when I still had my car I used to play it loud, I mean full blast. It always tore at my heart as I pictured the particular scene in the film, when Andrew who is dying of Aids realises that in the midst of all the suffering there is love. His understanding and love of the music moved him to tears as it does me.

By all accounts they serve champagne on the croquet lawn before Operatic performances at the Manor so that in itself seems quite wonderful. Yes, I might plan to go. After all, it is on a bus route! I recall that the grounds are spectacular too. It has yew hedges that are said to be the highest in England. Yes, I'm a bit of a one for remembering facts when I can barely recall where I left my house keys!

Through a pair of kissing gates I slipped further into the countryside. The vista of wide-open fields, trees and hedgerows made me wish I had my camera with me. You would have been in heaven, dear. I saw a buzzard quietly swoop past, hedgehopping. The sound of 'pee-yow' as it soared off, travelled eerily through the air. Nature satisfies my soul but after about an hour or so of wandering, I was ready to return to the warmth of the pub.

The Menu for my supper left me spoilt for choice. But I finally decided on the lamb shank in mint gravy. I wasn't disappointed. Afterwards, I ordered a pot of tea. I wanted to keep a clear head, ready for the ghost hunting!

So, Abbie, soon came the hour! When I left the pub, I felt both excited and somewhat apprehensive. The air was so still and there was a halo round the moon. The clouds had thickened and already the first snowflakes were falling silently to the ground. I shivered, but needs must! All around, the silence was almost overwhelming; that eeriness when you sense something is about to happen. The snow began to fall faster and thicker. Trees held their bare branches up offering themselves as fleeting carriers for the heaven sent flakes drifting down. The atmosphere was hushed except for my carefully planted footsteps.

Dusk, and a few late starlings joined the rest of the flock on the tower of the church, cawing noisily. I shivered, my nerves on edge. Inside the porch, I found shelter from the elements but it was rather dank and dark, scarily dark. The light above the porch was out. Only the moon occasionally appearing from behind a cloud shed light into the cavernous space. I stamped my feet upon the flagstones, trying to ease the cold that crept up through my body.

A bat suddenly plunged by and an owl hooted, swooping through the graveyard. The scene, reminiscent of a horror film made me tremble and sweat. Abbie, I expect you are wondering why I wasn't making my way back to the pub, well I can tell you, that's exactly what I was asking myself! Suddenly, ghost hunting had become a less than idyllic past-time.

I started to move, shoving my hands deep into my pockets. That's when the porch light flickered on and then off again. I became aware of a movement behind me, and a scraping, scratching sound on the floor. My head felt unusually wired. I put my hands over my ears, attempting to blot out the eerie jangle of whisperings and strange sounds pressing down. Then, a sudden blast of pungent air edged closer. With fear I turned slowly to face the noise. A figure of a hooded monk, bent over, bearing the countenance of someone very old, stood within touching distance. My legs were shaking and I could barely breathe as it moved closer. For a second I felt frozen to the spot before an adrenaline surge saw me moving as fast as I was able towards the lychgate. Yew trees dark and foreboding lined my way. The snow-covered flagstones were slippery under my feet and suddenly my arms flailed in the air as I was catapulted forward. "Steady," said a voice I recognised. You've guessed dear, the barman from the pub.

"Am I pleased to see you! I saw a ghost!" I told him, my heart racing.

"What here? I know one thing, you're shaking like a wet puppy."

I took his outstretched arm and leaned into him, suddenly not at all the brave, excitement seeking soul.

"My boss let me come to rescue you. I told her about the ghost you were hoping to see and she said I had misinformed you. It's not this church. There used to be a ghost at St Giles, Horspath, a local Parish, not here."

"I tell you. There is a ghost!" I replied. "A hunched over monk."

"A monk. You sure? The ghost at St Giles was supposed to be a monk. He hasn't been seen for years – just disappeared. Blimey, perhaps he came here!" he chortled.

"Don't make jokes. I can tell you don't believe me but then I can hardly believe what I witnessed either."

"Tell you what? Be good for trade, putting this story about."

"It's not a story," I shouted. "It's a fact. I saw a ghost." Honestly Abbie I thought I was going to die. The young man probably saw me as some old fool but he never said so. I told him I'd had enough excitement for one night and then he helped me back to the pub. The landlady apologised, saying the barman had given me the wrong information.

"Just like him," she muttered.

"It's not a problem. After all I shouldn't even be here," I said smiling, explaining about my journey to the village that morning.

"Oh well, must be a reason then."

"Yes, there was!"

After supping a stiff drink, given on the house, I headed for my bed. So Abbie, you probably won't believe me, about the ghost and all that, but that's my latest adventure! Time to have one of your own as I keep telling you!

Take care dearest and hope to see you soon.

Love Aunt Bella.

Dear Aunt Bella. She would be thrilled to hear about my adventure and the White Lady! I decided to give her a call and invite her over.

Aiden and Aunt Bella visited a few days later. Aunt Bella looked amazing, pink hair and all! The most positive person I knew, she listened attentively to my recent foray into having an adventure of my own.

"Perhaps you need to see where that story ends?" she queried with a smile.

"Maybe. I am thinking about it," I replied.

Aiden looked aghast. He couldn't comprehend why.

"You met a stranger and you want to see him again? Suppose you think he might be the one eh?"

I looked away and winked at Aunt Bella. She smiled back.

"Ladies. Love stories with happy endings happen in films. They are not real life. You can't go around trusting everyone you meet."

"Not everyone. Just someone," I said, "Come on Aunt Bella help me out."

"Well dear. Trust your instincts. Listen to your heart."

The trouble was I had trusted my instincts before and look where that got me. Perhaps I should remember one of Aunt Bella's other sayings instead – Holiday romances are never the same when you get home. They always disappoint!

"Anyway Abbie, on a positive note I think you've done wonders here. It now looks lived in. Not in a cluttered, chaotic manner, in a comfy way," said Aiden.

"Here here," said Aunt Bella. All you need now is a job and you will be settled. Have you started looking?"

"I have but I'm thinking about going freelance instead. Give me more independence and opportunity."

"More travelling?" asked Aunt Bella.

"Not for a while. My experience in the States took a lot out of me. I'm still in the recovery stage," I said feigning collapse.

"Talking of America. Gosh, I nearly forgot. A letter came to my place yesterday addressed to you. Sorry, I should have mentioned it straightaway," said Aiden, delving into his pocket before handing me an envelope.

At once I knew who sent it - Mike.

I quickly read it through and then folded it up and placed it back in the envelope.

"So, what does he want this time? I presume it's your old friend. Whatever it is, please say, No!"

I looked across at Aiden. Shuffling my feet I told him that Mike was apologising for what happened on my last visit.

"He wants me to go over. I think I should. In the letter he says we never got chance to discuss anything last time. We need to clear the air. I can't move on with my life until I know for sure how we both feel. What do you think Aunt Bella?"

"Well, I think it's your decision. Just be careful dear. You've been hurt enough already. I mean…."

"Am I the only one that sees clearly these days? Tear the letter up. I wish I hadn't given it to you now. He's just messing with your head and your affections, can't you see that?"

Shaking my head, I justified Mike's actions. "Mostly, it was his father's fault. He was always at his beck and call. Mike tried to please him."

"Like father like son. But, it's up to you. Go if you must. Only, don't say I didn't warn you."

I managed to book a last minute round trip for the following day with a return date two weeks later. Unable to face any more home truths, and a little anxious about the decision I'd made, I decided not to ask Aiden to look after Bailey. Aiden would only have picked up on my unease and make me cancel everything. I asked Aunt Bella instead. She was more than happy to come and stay at my place and look after Bailey.

A taxi arrived to take me to the Airport. Bailey pawed at my bags and leapt up to lick me, almost knocking me off my feet. I leant down to kiss his whiskery muzzle, tears in my eyes. With her arm around me, Aunt Bella consoled me, saying she would take very good care of him. Then she made such a fuss of Bailey, he didn't even bother to see me off!

In his letter Mike stated that Vanessa was a big mistake and begged for my forgiveness. Vanessa came along at a time when I was weakest, he had written. He didn't say when. Still, at least he had admitted something. A pretty girl like Vanessa would have been hard to ignore. The idea that their relationship had led to an engagement made me uneasy though. Probably because a marriage proposal, a ring, they were events I had only dreamt of. Mike had never proposed to me, I thought sadly. And I would have shouted, yes, yes, yes!

The flight was smooth, yet I was too unsettled to sleep, even after a couple of drinks. I read a novel, briefly, watched a film, fleetingly, and then simply gazed out the window. The sky was a clear azure blue. Mid Atlantic, clouds gathered, but not enough to cause any turbulence. For work commitments I travelled business class. On this occasion my seat in World Traveller Plus was comfortable and still provided meals and bar service. People watching passed some of the time; it's amazing what travellers get up to on a seven-hour flight! One 'gentleman' and a passenger across the aisle became very animated and enamoured with one another. Halfway through the flight she was diving underneath a blanket he draped around the two of them!

The Captain announced the weather in Philadelphia was clear and bright. Then in no time at all the city skyline beckoned. We descended over the wide Delaware River, the industrial areas and the Naval Dockyard before grass rushed beneath us, swiftly followed by the runway. We landed with an almighty bump but even that couldn't keep pace with my heart, which was pounding. Eager to disembark, I released my seatbelt, grabbed my hand luggage and shoved my way along the aisle, apologising profusely.

Waiting at the carousel for my luggage took an age. My patience had worn thin. What if my coming back turned out to be a huge mistake, proving my brother right? On the other hand, coming to Philly again might give me everything and more than I'd ever dreamt of. I needed to stay focused and positive.

On this occasion Mike appeared totally overjoyed

to see me. He spun me round and held me tight. "I wasn't sure you would come over," he said.

"Well, I'm here now. But, seriously, we do need to talk."

"Sure. Let's get ourselves sorted at the hotel first and then we can go and eat. OK?"

"Yes, sounds great," I replied, smiling.

We checked into The Ritz Carlton. No expense had been spared. The penthouse suite in the hotel was beautiful with spectacular views of City Hall. But feeling a little uneasy, bearing in mind how things had been on my last visit, I asked Mike to give me some time to freshen up and change. He said not to rush, to take my time and meet him in the Club Lounge on the top floor in an hour, as he needed to make a few business calls anyway.

Walking around the suite, I could barely believe what I saw. There was a separate dining space with seating for eight, a living room, plus a second bedroom, bathroom and kitchen. Indeed, the suite was far larger than the whole of my brother's house.

After an enjoyable soak in the marble bathroom, I wrapped myself in a huge fluffy bath sheet and sat on the bed staring at the stunning view. I felt like an alien from another planet in such a place so unlike back home. Still, surely it was something I could get used to!

I chose a close-fitting blue linen dress and jacket from the closet. It looked very elegant without being too fussy; an outfit for best, Aunt Bella might say. A couple of months earlier, we went shopping together and she had persuaded me to buy it. At the time, I wondered if I'd ever actually have an occasion to wear it. At home casual clothing was more me. Now when

I looked in the full-length mirror, I hardly recognised myself; fully made up, black tights and heels, all quite a change from my usual attire. To be honest though, I looked uncomfortable. Turning away from the mirror, I checked my watch, straightened my shoulders and took a deep breath before I headed off to the lounge.

Mike was sitting opposite the door at a table for two. The minute I entered, he got up to greet me. He was the old Mike, the one I had fallen in love with, smiling and relaxed.

"An iconic and beautiful view for a beautiful lady," he said.

"The view is pretty special, I will grant you that."

"I've ordered sangria and some of their speciality Goldenberg peanut chews to savour. Thought we could have a meal a bit later in the restaurant."

"Looks like you've taken care of everything!"

"That's the Boss in me I guess," Mike grinned.

My tummy gave a nervous dance.

"How was your flight?"

"Smooth, but interesting," I replied.

Mike nodded and looked thoughtful. The elephant in the room overshadowed the need for small talk.

"I think we need to get 'the business' out of the way first," Mike said.

To start with, he acknowledged that he had never stood up to his father and disliked the way they had both treated me. As I thought, my time in the company came to an end at his father's bidding. Basically, his father had someone different in mind to become Mike's wife and it made life simpler if they let me go.

His reasons unleashed a tide of anger within me.

"You must have known how much that hurt. You said nothing. Taken you long enough to apologise hasn't it? Have you any idea how humiliated I felt?"

"What can I say?" he replied.

"Sorry! Try that for a start."

"Abbie, I have apologised. Albeit, not to your face. Please forgive me. Father controlled everything."

"Your heart too? Did he? And Vanessa? Well, I'm surprised he picked out someone so young."

"Oh, Vanessa. She wasn't his choice. Don't be silly. Vanessa was whom I fell in love with! Well, when I say 'fell in love with,' what I mean is, Vanessa and I had fun. Heady with lust we exchanged rings but we never married! Oh no! In lust perhaps, but no, never love. I met her before my father had chance to marry me off!"

Shocked, I shuffled uncomfortably in my chair. "I never thought you were that shallow," I said, my voice as cold as ice. I was seeing another side of Mike and it was one I didn't like at all.

Mike reached across the table for my hand. I pulled away.

"Don't be like that Abbie. Like I said. Vanessa was a just bit of fun. She meant nothing. Now, I want the whole shebang; wife, children, house in the country."

"So why did you get in touch with me then?"

"Because I need you Abbie. I've always needed you but I was too stupid to realise."

It didn't make any sense. Children, he said, children. What was he thinking?

I looked away. Mike put his hands up in surrender.

"Tell me how to convince you Abbie."

I looked him up and down. He didn't have a hair out of place. His beautifully manicured nails, gold diamond studded cuff links, tailored suit and designer shirt, they all reeked of money. Trouble was, he could buy anything he wanted. And, the children, well he needed someone to pass all his wealth down to, I thought cynically.

"Don't look so frightened. I will wait. I expect this has all come as a huge shock. But believe me, it's you that I love."

"Children? You said children."

"Yes Abbie. Surrogacy. Honestly, I've worked it all out. Vanessa has agreed."

I stood up, reached across and slapped Mike straight across the cheek. "How dare you!" I spat.

"Listen, Abbie. We can work it out."

With that he grabbed my hands and kissed me. Then, I knew for certain. I stood erect and stared straight into his eyes. I rubbed my mouth with the back of my hand. Mike stuttered and I put my finger to his lips and shushed him.

"Now, it's my turn. You see I'm not the person I used to be," I said sternly. "While you've been trying to sort your future out, so have I. This isn't what I want. All this, isn't what I need," I continued, casting my arm out around the room. "Materialism is not important or attractive to me. So, yes, it's my turn to say sorry. Sorry that you have wasted your time. And, trust me. You can't buy love. Love grows when and where you least expect it. Certainly not here on the fortieth floor."

For on the top of that building in Philadelphia, the City of Love, I knew this wasn't where I was meant to be. Mike was flabbergasted. He had no answers. The look in his eyes said it all. He was angry. Before he had time to challenge me, I turned and walked away towards the elevator, to head to the Penthouse.

I didn't have much to pack as I had intended to buy a whole new wardrobe during my visit. But, I didn't need to. All I wanted was back home.

During the return flight a sense of ease came over me, in spite of realising what a fool I'd been, daydreaming about my lost love from New Jersey. Perhaps he never was 'my love' any way, just a romantic notion. True love wasn't that deluded, self-seeking, self-obsessed feeling. Surely, when you truly loved someone, you allowed them freedom and choice. You allowed them to discover who they really wanted to be; not an imitation of oneself. Perhaps, now I loved myself enough to do that! Yes, long lasting love meant compassion, respect, desire and living the dream together. Being in someone else's shadow wasn't love. Only now was the balancing act making sense.

Relationships, good relationships make you proud to be with that certain someone. When you go somewhere without them you constantly wish they were with you. You miss them. In the past, perhaps I had been guilty of accepting the love I thought I deserved. Now, I wanted respect, compassion and to see desire when that certain, special someone looked at me.

Chapter 8

It was late summer. After a great deal of soul searching, I decided to go with Aunt Bella's earlier advice, "Follow your heart." I didn't dare tell Aiden.

On the deck stood pots of bright red geraniums, blue lobelia and white bocapa. The pale grey window boxes were alight and alive with colourful pansies; their pretty faces jostling with each other. The veranda looked so welcoming. It was a perfect spot to sit with a cup of coffee on such a beautiful, sunny day. The door to the cottage was ajar but disappointingly, just as on my very first visit, Bill didn't appear to be in. I decided to take a stroll down the garden.

That's when I saw him! Bill was facing away from me, busy feeding the chickens. I stood for some time, just watching. When he turned sideways I realised he no longer had his beard. Pity, he looked rugged and more handsome with his beard. All the same, he looked pretty good anyway.

"Chook, chook, come on Betsey," Bill cooed, sprinkling grain onto the dry ground.

"You too Abbie. Come on, eat up before she

devours it all."

Oh my goodness. Bill had named a chicken after my beloved car and another after me! Dressed casually in jeans tucked into his wellingtons, a thick jumper that was the colour of dirty pastry and an old flat cap on his head, he was the picture of a comfortably dressed yokel! (The complete opposite of Mike in all his dandy finery.) I didn't have Bailey with me this time to give me away with his frantic barking, yanking on his lead to get closer. Even so, I had to stop myself from yelping out Bill's name. I was so pleased to see him.

When Bill turned towards me, a glint of summer sun captured his gaze for a moment. For a few seconds he couldn't see me. When he did, with arms outstretched, he literally ran, his boots clump, clumping on the ground. He looked like a son running towards his mother at the end of his first day at school; as a man returning home after the war; as a hopeful lover.

"I thought you would never come!" Bill said. "I……"

Before he managed to utter another word I pressed my mouth on his, silencing him. When our lips parted, Bill said, "You didn't forget me then?"

"No, you've been with me all the while. Dear Bill, forgive me for taking so long deciding what to do and coming to my senses."

"I don't think you are capable of ever coming to your senses Abbie! But dear Princess, there is nothing to forgive."

We talked and talked until we were hoarse. Bill made a lovely meal and we sat together in front of the fire to eat. (Who needs a dining table big enough for a dozen to sit round when you can have such closeness?) We drank wine, more than we should, and by midnight we were falling asleep in our chairs. Bill shook me and said perhaps we had better go upstairs. Hesitantly, I agreed to share the same bed. But I need not have worried. As soon as our heads hit the pillows, we fell fast asleep.

When I came down to breakfast the following morning, straightaway, I sensed something was wrong; there was an atmosphere in the air. Bill was making a pot of tea but he never as much as looked when he heard me enter the room. He wasn't singing or whistling as he usually did either. The fire had died right down; it was cold.

"Whatever is the matter?" I asked, nervously.

"Abbie, I can't do this. Sorry, I just can't."

I walked over to him and touched his sleeve. He held my hand and then very gently pushed me away.

"Bill, please. Please, don't do this. Tell me what is wrong. Please," I begged.

"I'm sorry. I really don't have the capacity to love again." He slowly turned away and headed for the door. "Please just go. Be gone when I return. Please."

When Bill closed the door behind him I crumpled in a heap. He couldn't love me? And that was before I told him all about myself. Perhaps he had already guessed my reluctance to get too close.

Our relationship had been a wonderful friendship. Yes, we had kissed but never gone further. Oh, but how I had wanted to be held in a loving embrace. More than that, with my very being I still wanted to be held in Bill's strong arms and be loved. I didn't want for anything more. Looking around the room my heart sank. This was where we had talked of making our own memories. I looked at the fireside chair and thought of Bill sitting there. Like the chair, my life would be so empty without him.

An hour later and my bags are packed and standing by the door. But I wasn't leaving without the chance of a proper goodbye. When Bill returned and saw me, he shook with such emotion. He struggled to look at me or speak. "Why didn't you just go?" he asked, sadly.

"Because I need to know why you are turning me away. I thought this was our perfect chance of happiness and for my own sanity, I must know what I did wrong."

We sat together in the sitting room. At first there was a deathly silence between us. Then I reached for Bill's hand, turned the palm over and kissed it. Bill wept.

"Alice. When she died my heart broke. I can't take the worry of that happening again. If I lost you......"

"Bill, dear Bill. Listen. Sometimes we have to take a risk in life before we realise what we are capable of. You said some time ago, Alice would want you to be happy. So, let's make her happy too. I can't replace her Bill, but I need you as much as you need me. Let's try."

At that very moment, Strangers in the night by Frank Sinatra came on the radio.

"I love this song. That's what we were. Remember? But we are not strangers now, are we?" I whispered.

Bill looked at me lovingly. "No, we are certainly not. I was just scared. More than that, terrified. But like you said, we need each other. I'm willing to give it my best shot. How about you?"

"I think you already know my answer. It's a resounding yes please. But…."

At this point, I knew the whole truth about me had to come out.

Looking down, not wanting to see the reaction on his face, I started to share my story. "There's something you have to know. I've, I've…." I stuttered.

"Well, as we've agreed we are more than strangers and perhaps, hope to be more than friends, whatever it is shouldn't make any difference. I mean, if you have a history of sheep stealing or a dozen children to come and live with us, or a dog that rolls in dung then flops on my sofa, I don't care. I don't care what you have. Ok?" he replied light-heartedly.

"Stop joking! It's not what I have Bill. It's what's missing - what I don't have. For starters there cannot be any children in my life."

"Why? You are young. Oh, sorry, you mean you can't *have* children? No matter. We can still have a full life together, or adopt if we decide children need to be part of our family.

"No listen. Please Bill, just, listen. It's not that. I can't have children because I've had cancer."

There was a nanosecond of silence before Bill replied. "You poor girl. Come here."

My tears dampened his sweater as I buried my face in his chest. My body shook with sobs as I tried to catch my breath. Bill stroked my hair and said gently, "So, you've had a hysterectomy? That doesn't change how I feel about you."

I looked up into his face.

"Don't look so afraid," Bill said, kissing my

forehead.

Still crying, I slowly shook my head. "No, it's not that. I haven't had a hysterectomy. But like I said, I've had cancer." I swallowed hard before continuing. "For six months I went back and forth to see my GP. He prescribed antibiotics, claiming I had an infection. My symptoms didn't improve but I was told I was worrying about a disease I did not have. At my fourth appointment within a few weeks I was prescribed antidepressants. Did they work their magic? No! Eventually, I paid privately to have a mammogram and other tests – ones that the GP said were unnecessary. The results came back positive; I had cancer."

"Abbie, I am so sorry."

"Let me finish," I said softly. "I had a mastectomy. Afterwards, I was advised that a pregnancy and the hormonal changes might increase a risk of re-occurrence. In time the risk lessens but I won't take that chance. Plus, having such a dread of hospitals, I also refused breast reconstruction. To be free from cancer I've accepted my loss. I will never change my mind. I've had enough of hospitals to last a lifetime. So, you see – I'm not whole and I will never be a mother. As well as being scatty, I'm lopsided too!" (This last sentence was meant to be a bit of a joke but neither of us did as much as smile.) "I'm sure this will change everything. That's why I waited so long before telling you."

Bill disentangled me from his arms and got up. Slowly he walked over to the window. The air was still between us. I held my breath. Then, Bill's shoulders heaved before a deep sob and almost a scream left his throat. He was holding onto the windowsill for support. As his crying lessened he slowly turned to face me.

Bill's face looked so drawn and sad. Walking towards me, he dabbed his eyes with his sleeve. I dreaded what he was going to say. He needed to be honest, but I wasn't sure that I could face what was coming. I had taken a gamble and I was scared of the outcome. What if it meant I lost this person who had become so dear to me.

The corner of Bill's mouth twitched before he spoke. He looked as nervous as I felt. Just say it, I wanted to shout – get it over with! I was unprepared for what he said.

"Abbie, you beautiful, silly, courageous woman. It doesn't matter one jot! I'm sad that you went through so much, that's why I'm upset. But I still want you, really want you. Can't you see the pleasure in my eyes when I look at you? I love you with all of my heart. Nothing, and I mean nothing, will ever change that."

I looked up at this very special man standing in front of me. He was kind, thoughtful, sensitive and caring. He made a mean omelette too! And he truly loved me. I put my arms out towards him and he held my hands before gently pulling me up from the sofa. Falling into his arms, I felt treasured. When he swept me up in one swift movement I gasped, with pure longing. As he carried me up the stairs to the bedroom my heart raced, beating with excitement and resolution and some trepidation. This was the moment I had both feared and looked forward to.

Bill carefully lowered me onto the bed then lay down beside me. We kissed tenderly, holding one another close. As our lips parted, Bill gently lifted my sweater. I shuddered in ecstasy as he made little butterfly kisses across my stomach. When he moved up to my neckline, before playfully nibbling at my ear, I thought I was going to faint. Then he kissed me again, full on the mouth, with passion.

Half sitting propped on one elbow, I tried to take my sweater off. I started to giggle at my clumsiness. Bill smiled before helping me. "Take it easy, there is no rush," he said patiently.

I sat up and carefully unhooked my bra. Letting it fall softly onto the bed-cover, my prosthesis fully hidden inside, I looked up at Bill. Love shone in his eyes, still. Pushing my shoulders, he very cautiously eased me back down onto the bed and then leaned down to kiss my mastectomy scar.

"You truly are a beautiful woman," he whispered.

I was lost for words. He had said I was beautiful - a beautiful woman. There was nothing else he needed to say.

The next day we had lots of talking to do and somewhat difficult decisions to make. Did I want to get a job locally, which meant we could live at the Hideaway together or, should we take things a bit slower? I could work from my rented cottage in Hampshire and visit Bill at weekends.

"What are we waiting for?" Bill asked. "Do we need to ease ourselves in gently? I'm ready for a change, a long-term change. Yes, I'm up for getting on with the rest of my life. A life with you in it, Miss Bennett!"

Smiling, I nodded, "Me too. Oh, but I do have one condition. Do you think you might like to grow your beard again?"

Bill chuckled. "Only on the condition that a

whiskery fella called Bailey will be living here too!"

"Sure thing," I said, grinning from ear to ear.

"What I must do is go and see Aiden. Perhaps you could come too?"

"OK. Lets hope he gives his approval. Why don't you go back and give him the heads up, then I'll come up in a week or so."

"You're not getting cold feet, are you Bill?" I said nervously. "I'm sure Aiden will be delighted to have someone else fussing over me. He's probably tired of hopelessly trying to figure me out."

"Even so, if you don't mind Abbie. Give me a chance to get this cottage sorted before you move in permanently. Fix it up a little."

"Don't change a thing. I love it! And in time, if we think something needs doing, let's do it together, shall we?"

Bill nodded slowly in agreement.

"But, I'd still like to leave it a couple of days. Get the chickens sorted, you know how it is."

"Um, alright. Promise you will use that relic of a mobile and call me though?"

"I will, scouts honour," Bill replied, holding up three fingers in salute.

The next morning I set off. Smiling, I thought about how I was going to tell Aiden my news. Goodness knows what he might say. Still, it was my decision. At least the United States no longer figured in my plans.

Throughout my journey back to Hampshire, I thought about Aiden's possible reaction to my news. His questioning would be thorough and the answers might elude me. Perhaps, I'd say, yes I had a lovely time and leave it at that to start with. Bill, was used to interrogation, he could deal with Aiden! Once they met, Aiden would see how sincere he was. Trouble was, I needed to convince Aiden to meet Bill. Just as well I had a few days to do that. Otherwise I stood to lose the man I wanted to spend the rest of my life with.

Aunt Bella. She told me to follow my heart. Perhaps if she visited at the same time the atmosphere would be less strained. Aiden wanted to protect me, no harm in that, but he safeguarded me too much sometimes. Probably because I had made so many mistakes in the past! But, Aunt Bella's diplomacy and life experiences meant she'd be able to mediate wisely. And, hopefully, be on my side!

I called Aunt Bella when I reached Aiden's house.

"Of course, dear, I'd love to meet your beau."

"Beau, that sounds romantic."

"Affairs of the heart call for romance. There's nothing sterile about a lifelong love affair," she said softly.

"On that note, how's Malcolm?" I queried.

"He's fine. We still see each other, periodically. A meal, a chat, you know."

"I don't need to buy a new hat?"

"No dear. That will never happen. I love my independence too much."

"Aiden does too. Still, one day, some lovely woman will sweep him off his feet and then the matter of independence will get overshadowed. Least, that's what I hope."

"Abbie, not everyone needs someone to make them happy. You like being part of a couple. Some of us love our freedom too much to give long-term relationships a chance. Give Aiden his due; he's perfectly content as he is."

"What a pity though. He's got a home with room to share!"

"Honestly, if that special person came along he'd be unable to resist. Love does that."

"Do you regret never marrying?"

"Not for a minute. I'd rather be content on my own than with the wrong person. I could never pretend to be happy if the person I was with bored the life out of me and sadly after a time I believe that might happen. I'm just not cut out for happy ever afters. Plus, at my age, I'm not cut out for anything more than a kiss goodnight if you get my drift."

"Aunt Bella! Really!"

"So this new beau, man friend, does he make your heart race? Do you miss him already?"

"Yes, and Yes. I've never felt so comfortable with anyone. He's special."

"Then, I'm glad dear. You deserve that."

"Wait till you meet him. His hazel eyes are so dreamy, you get lost in them. And, he loves me, little old me!" I gasped.

"Well, I will look forward to sizing him up. Give me a call when you're ready. Have you told him about me?"

"Of course. Told him how eccentric and fascinating you are and how much I love you."

"That's nice! Don't put me on a pedestal though as I'm likely to fall. My imperfections are almost perfect these days. The saying, *Imperfection is beauty, madness is genius and it's better to be absolutely ridiculous than absolutely boring,* that's me, don't you think?"

"Absolutely! When you meet Bill, be all of that. He's kind, thoughtful, funny and I know you will love him. There's nothing not to like. Why don't you come for a few days and really get to know him."

"I suppose that's a good idea. Plus, there's nothing in my diary till next month. Then, I'm off to see the Northern Lights. A new adventure."

"Oh, that will be amazing. Can I come too if I can tear myself away from 'my beau,' Aunt Bella?"

"Maybe. You see Malcolm has booked this trip too."

"Well, I'm not playing gooseberry!"

Aunt Bella was full of surprises. Didn't she say they saw one another periodically for a chat and a drink? Perhaps she fancied him more than she let on. Although, a companion for holidays sounded a fitting arrangement, perfectly suited to Aunt Bella.

Aiden took my news somewhat soberly. Perhaps, he sensed my relationship with Bill was different; that it mattered. Surprisingly, he even told me to invite Bill to stay as soon as possible.

"What's the rush? Of course you need to meet him but it's not like you. I mean, despite my invitations to get you to come to the States, you never did. Mike handled you not being keen but to be honest I felt shunned."

"Sorry Abbie. Coming meant giving my approval. I only spoke to him once on the phone and he sounded a real jerk! Kept going on about how he had changed you. Made you into someone respected in your field."

"Did he indeed! That was not his doing. I earned respect. He always needed to promote himself by any means available. But using me, that's unforgiveable. You should have said."

"Honestly Abbie. At that time you probably would not have listened, let alone agreed he was a real jerk!"

"Umm, maybe not. Still, I'm glad you've enlightened me. There is not an ounce of me that misses him now."

Bill called, as promised. We arranged a full weekend together.

"I'm nervous Abbie. What if they don't like me? What if I bore the pants off them? Hell, what if I don't like them?"

"You don't need to worry about a thing. It's not going to be two worlds colliding or a horrid interview for a job. It's one person meeting the other two people I adore. What could possibly go wrong?"

Saturday morning, I got up early. "Bill is coming to see us," I told Bailey, full of excitement. Bailey leapt up, sensing my mood, placing his paws on my shoulders. He gazed deep into my eyes, rapt with devotion.

"Too much," I said, turning my face away from his affectionate licking. "Momma needs to get ready."

I was just dabbing a bit of lipstick on when I heard the front door bell. I dashed to the window just in time to see a taxi heading back down the drive.

"I'll go. Aunt Bella's arrived," I shouted to Aiden, before rushing downstairs. Breathless with anticipation, I opened the door, and then gasped.

"What are you doing?" I asked, my voice shaking.

"You never gave me your forwarding address; you blocked my phone and so Honey, here I am," Mike said, grinning from ear to ear.

I looked him up and down. Dressed in suit, shirt and tie, he resembled a salesman. He stood on the doorstep like a Jehovah Witness, keen to engage.

"Why now?" I asked forcibly.

Aiden came rushing to see the cause of all the commotion. Bailey peeped out round the corner of the doorjamb, before wrinkling his nose and baring his teeth. It was so unlike him.

"What's going on?" Aiden shouted. "Whatever you are selling we don't want or need it. Look, on the door, 'No cold callers. Thank you."

"I'm not here to sell you anything. I'm Mike. You must be Aiden," Mike replied, holding out his hand.

Aiden turned to me, "What's going on?" he queried.

"I have no idea. But, I want him to go."

"Well, you heard what she said. My sister wants you to leave."

"But, Abigail, Abbie honey, let me explain, please."

Down the drive came Bill in his 4 x 4. Bailey recognised the sound of his vehicle and rushed out to greet him, his tail waving madly, his tongue lolling out the side of his mouth.

"This might be interesting," quipped Aiden, as Mike turned to see who was approaching the house.

Bill's face looked a picture of bewilderment. He stepped out of the car and waved while Bailey cavorted round his feet. "Surely, this welcoming party isn't for me?" he teased.

"And you are?" interrupted Mike, stepping forward.

"Bill, I'm here to meet Aiden."

"Well, get in line!" said Mike, full of arrogance.

"Mike, I think it best you leave, don't you?" I said. "Before things get out of hand. You're not welcome."

Bill looked totally confused.

"Honey," Mike continued, "we need to talk. Just you and me."

"We said everything we needed to last time we met," I replied, linking my arm through Bill's.

Mike straightened his shoulders and stood tall. "I don't want any trouble. I just need to speak to Abbie, it's important."

Aiden stepped in front of Mike and spoke clearly and loudly, "Nothing is more important to me right now than seeing you off these premises. You really are overstepping the mark by hanging around. Do I make myself clear?"

Mike's shoulders slumped. I had never seen him look so worried. I touched his arm gently and said, "I'm sorry."

Bill looked at me and I took his hand. "Tell him Bill, please."

"I'm sorry Mike but the lady has made up her mind. I know it's hard when you loose someone. But you had your chance Mate and you blew it. Be best if you go now."

Aiden stood with his fists clenched. He looked furious as he turned to give Mike another piece of his mind. "Got the message, go. I can order a taxi if you like or you can walk. Its some distance to the town but give you chance to clear your head."

"Abbie?"

I shook my head. "It's over Mike. Trust me."

Mike looked beaten. "Incompatible, that's what we are," I said softly. "You said it yourself, remember?"

Mike turned on his heels and slowly walked away, back down the drive. No one followed, not even Bailey. Aiden and Bill walked into the house, chatting like long, lost friends.

Ten minutes later Aunt Bella arrived. I flung my arms around her and cried, letting go of all the pent-up emotion.

"Whatever has happened?" she said.

Between sobs I managed to tell her.

"So was it almost pistols at dawn?" she joked.

"Something like that. I thought Aiden was going to punch him!"

"And now you feel guilty? Abbie dear, did you ask him to fly over here? Did your heart go all a flutter when you saw him?"

I shook my head.

"Well then, stop blaming yourself. I want to see the man who makes you happy. So now dry your eyes and take me to meet him. "

Bill and Aiden had busied themselves making lunch. A spread was laid out on the table in the kitchen. As Aunt Bella and I walked in, they were clinking glasses, "To Abbie and happiness."

"What about us?" I asked. "Aunt Bella and I need a drink."

"Ah, you must be Bill," said Aunt Bella. Then she turned to me and whispered, "I see what you mean, hazel and dreamy."

I smiled, then walked across to Bill and kissed him, passionately.

"Get a room!" Aiden interrupted, slapping Bill on his back.

A couple of days afterwards, I headed back to Bill at The Hideaway. The last of days of summer welcomed me, as did Bill with open arms. With the idea of sharing my life with such a special person, I could not have been happier.

Once my belongings arrived, I nestled a few photos alongside Bills; a photo of Aunt Bella and my brother, I took over to the dresser. That's when I noticed the framed picture of Alice had been moved.

"Bill, where's the photo of Alice?" I asked.

"Thought it best to put it away," Bill replied.

"Why?"

"Well, you know. Part of the past."

"A happy piece. Please have the photo out. I've got one of my Mum and Dad. They won't get shut away. We can't be jealous of those who are no longer here, can we?"

"You are amazing. Alice would have liked you. I'll put her photo in the spare bedroom."

"Good. We will create our own special memories too. I think this is the beginning of something quite wonderful."

The double wedding ring quilt on our bed complemented the floral wallpaper that we chose for our bedroom. We looked forward to having a fire burning in the fireplace on cold wintery nights. I imagined the flickering flames casting shadows around the room as we snuggled down together, with Bailey sprawled across the rug alongside Bill. Bailey had hardly left his side since we arrived.

With the last fix of sunshine before the nights draw in we decided to hold a party. Bill called it a 'welcome home, house warming party'. We invited Aiden and Aunt Bella of course, and a couple of Bill's old colleagues from work who were thrilled with Bill's news. Julie, the barmaid from our local haunt had become one of my dearest friends. She introduced us to people who we now see regularly at the pub, so they've had their invites too. They told us they had never heard of The Hideaway, but I said, it's not that difficult to find!!

In preparation for the party, I got my sewing machine out for the first time in years, keen to be the little homemaker. Feeling industrious, I made yards and yards of pretty bunting to pin up along the veranda to welcome our friends. With fairy lights round the front door, pots of chrysanthemums on the whitewashed deck, colourful throws on the wicker furniture, it all looked very attractive. The Hideaway had woken up and come alive.

Before everyone arrived, we lit candles in coloured glass jam jars and hung them in the boughs of an old apple tree. Then Bill set to and swept away fallen leaves by the steps, nodding in approval at the scene. An old tin bath held bottles of beer and wine. I was just heating a rabbit casserole and a venison stew when our first visitors arrived; Aiden and Aunt Bella.

"I can see the attraction in moving here, Abbie," said Aunt Bella, straightaway. "Look at it, the countryside is stunning. In many ways it reminds me of when I lived out in the wilds in a little shack, years ago. Do you remember when you used to visit?"

"So, that's what The Hideaway reminded me of! First time I saw it, I felt reminded of somewhere from childhood. Now I realise. Your place had a veranda out the back too, didn't it?"

"Yes. You were only small when your parents used to visit with you two monkeys in tow! Your Mum never understood how I managed to live in the middle of nowhere, but I loved it. The solitude of being alone without being lonely gave me time to reflect, an opportunity to get away from distractions. Ah yes…chance to dream," she said wistfully.

Bill nodded. "Sometimes you need that break, that freedom," he said. "In the hub-bub of every day life, its difficult finding a little space to call your own. Until, that is, a special someone comes along to share it with you." He turned to me and winked.

"It's delightful. I'm sure Abbie will be very happy here," said Aiden, giving Bill his customary slap on the back before coming over to hug me.

"Yes, I love everything about this place. Most especially the owner," I replied, smiling.

Our friends and Bill's former colleagues arrived and they were all taken in by our home.

"It must feel like you are on holiday all the year round living here," one of them said.

"Oh, but it does," I cooed in agreement.

"I'm so happy for you Bill," said Dave, a former colleague. You look well. Living here suits you."

"I went through some tough times but yes, this is contentment. My life now, I wouldn't change it for the world."

After a brief tour round the cottage, everyone settled themselves out on the veranda. Bill served drinks and Aunt Bella joined me in the kitchen. Through the open door I heard Bill catching up on news from his former colleagues. For me, having summer parties outside and gatherings inside in the winter was something to look forward to. This was my happy place.

After our main course, which was thoroughly enjoyed by all, I brought out an apple crumble and my prized sticky toffee pudding with jugs of custard. Bill was telling our friends about my first visit to the cottage. He told them I had a terrified look on my face when I saw him with his war wound and how he had banged his rifle on the floor making me jump. Soon, everyone was laughing hysterically.

"Now, before we dive into these scrumptious deserts there is something I need to do," Bill said. "So without further ado, darling will you come here for a moment."

I hadn't a clue about what he might say next, probably some joke about me running out of petrol or how he humped a can of fuel over the fields. I looked at him quizzically and he raised an eyebrow, a tell-tale sign he was about to say something teasing.

"Don't embarrass me Bill!" I told him as he put his arm around me and pulled me close.

"Me embarrass you. Hardly! No, what I want to say is something most of us already know. You saved me Abbie. I never realised just how alone I felt until I met you. Those months until you returned were some of the darkest days I've known. Inside I died a little more each day. But when you came back and I saw you standing at the top of the garden, my heart melted. There is no way I am ever going to let you escape again. And, remember how you said we had to take a risk. Well, I'm going to take my biggest gamble now."

Suddenly Bill was on one knee. He reached into

the inside pocket of his jacket and I covered my mouth and held my breath, my eyes on stalks. The ring he held cushioned in his hand was incredibly beautiful. He had shown it me once before; it had belonged to his dearest mother. I seemed to be in a trance for a moment or two until Bill's voice brought me back to earth with a softening bump.

"Dearest Princess, will you do me the honour of becoming my wife?"

"Yes please, yes please," I kept repeating, my head feeling lovely and fuzzy and my heart on fire for this man.

There were tears, there was laughter and congratulations, there was joy. When I began that journey to my weekend away in the country, almost nine months before, I could never have imagined what lie ahead.

Chapter 9

We planned our wedding for early summer the following year. Well, when I say planned, thankfully, there wasn't much to do. We wanted to keep it simple. The vicar in our local village said he'd be delighted to conduct the service in the church and we happily set the date and agreed to have the bells played before and after the ceremony. Aiden agreed to be Best Man and Aunt Bella was thrilled when I asked her to give me away. I intended to make my own bouquet and provide flowers for the church and Aunt Bella bravely volunteered to make our wedding cake. The reception was to take place at our home; our special place.

Choosing my dress for the occasion was difficult. Yes, I saw beautiful wedding dresses, but I had to take into account my previous surgery. It meant, low cut or off the shoulder styles were unsuitable. I mean, a low cut dress needed a cleavage, something I no longer had! The solution came when I discovered a beautiful, yet understated satin dress with narrow straps, which had a separate lace top with capped sleeves. The top was strewn with pearl beads and crystals in a delicate motif. The two together looked amazing. Once I'd made and stitched a pocket in the bodice into which I could pop a prosthesis, I knew the result would be perfect. To complete my ensemble, I purchased a cream top hat with a short mesh veil, strewn with tiny pearl beads.

The next few months went past in a whirl of activity. Together, Bill and I decorated several rooms in the cottage. Doing it was fun and helped the cottage become 'ours.' In the kitchen, the cupboards painted ivory, the wooden worktops sanded and oiled plus, new floral curtains, created a country style room with added character. Our bedroom became another beautiful space. It didn't need much attention; a freshen up of the paintwork mainly and although I loved the warm tone of the floorboards, two fluffy rugs each side of the bed stopped my sharp intake of breath on cold mornings! We also tidied up the huge barn at the bottom of the garden. Bill had dumped anything surplus to his immediate requirements in there when he moved in and not looked at them since. Once boxes were sorted through, and some of it discarded, we realised what a huge useful space we had. All kinds of future plans came to the fore - a party den, a Man cave, even a holiday let. Reining in our enthusiasm, we decided to leave our plans on the table for the time being. We had our wedding to think of and wanted a project to get involved in together afterwards.

Aunt Bella came to stay overnight before our big day. Her support was very welcome. We made a good team, baking cakes, pastries and scones for the buffet, a proper English cream tea. The weather was sunny and warm, just perfect for the planned reception. Bill had spent time tending the garden and planted it up with beautiful seasonal flowers and placed lovely hanging baskets around the veranda. We had wanted colourful and they were certainly that – bright blue lobelia, scarlet geraniums and scented petunias in every hue. Overflowing pots of pink and white fuchsias lined the steps to the deck, which was adorned with fairy lights and candles in jars. On the veranda, wicker chairs, bamboo seats and deckchairs added to the mixed relaxed mood that I wanted to create.

On the morning of the wedding, a delivery of fresh blooms arrived. I'd chosen trumpet shaped lilies, long stemmed daises and agapanthus, the love flower, to make up my bouquet and a flower arrangement to go next to the altar in the church. With some fresh greenery from the garden, the result was lovely. Plus, the fragrance from the lilies and the drama from the agapanthus and the innocence of the daises, they all worked in harmony.

Once the floral display was ready, Aunt Bella and Bill dashed off to place it in the church. Meanwhile, I intended to have a welcome soak in the bath, a chance to relax and unwind.

"All done. They look perfect," said Aunt Bella on their return. "I will just get ready and then I can help you do your hair. I must say, you look amazingly calm, dear."

"My heart is clanging like a cymbal! Honestly, I can hardly believe I'm getting married! Aunt Bella, I'm getting married!" I screamed.

"It's just wonderful. A match made in heaven."

That brought a tear to my eye; wishing Mum and Dad were there to share my special day. Every little girl dreams of their dad walking them down the aisle.

"Only happy tears, Abbie," said Aunt Bella. She knew what I was thinking. "Your Dad would be so proud. And pleased to know his big sister is playing her part! Remember, punctuality was his thing. He'd be saying, *don't you be late now!*"

"He certainly would. Where's Bill?"

"Oh he's ready; booted and spurred! They're leaving any minute. Aiden said that Bill doesn't want you to get there ahead of him!"

"Well, isn't it tradition for a bride to be late? Perhaps, I'll keep him waiting, just a while. Truth is, I don't think I can!"

Aunt Bella helped me into my dress. I stood sideways and looked in the mirror and then leant forward to check. The bodice fitted perfectly. I had been worried it might gape and reveal the slight indentation on the upper portion of my chest. Normally, my loss was something I accepted to be rid of that horrible disease, but this was a special day after all and I wanted to look perfect.

"You look stunning," said Aunt Bella. "Such a beautiful bride. Bill is a very lucky man."

"We're both lucky. Like you said, a match made in heaven."

I took one last look in the full-length mirror. Yes, I looked every inch a woman, quite beautiful.

"Well dear, let's go and meet your potential husband, shall we?"

In the village, the bells rang out. Children waved as I stepped from the car. In the porch, the vicar hovered before making his way inside.

Aunt Bella smiled. "Ready?" she asked.

"More than," I replied.

Aunt Bella kissed my cheek. Then we made our

way slowly from the lychgate to the church. As we stood in the doorway, the vicar nodded and my choice of music, prelude from Te Deum, resounded through the church. I walked slowly up the aisle, Aunt Bella by my side, in time to the music. Bill faced ahead, only turning to see me at the very last moment. Then, he gasped, before a tear trickled down his cheek.

Saying our wedding vows was truly special. When the vicar announced we were man and wife, our eyes locked, hypnotised. Finding one another was such a blessing and our marriage cemented our love. Our friends and Aiden and Aunt Bella applauded, as we walked back down the aisle to Ed Sheeran's 'thinking out loud.'

The lyrics made us smile –

"I'm thinking 'bout how people fall in love in mysterious ways,

Maybe just the touch of a hand…"

Once the customary wedding photos had been taken we headed back to The Hideaway. Right from the start, that's where we wanted to hold our reception; in the place where we met, where friendship blossomed, where love took hold, where Bailey looked happiest!

The reception was so relaxed and informal. We danced the whole night long to music, barefooted on the lawn. We weren't the only ones who danced all night. Aiden and Julie, the barmaid from the local pub hit it off at first sight! It was wonderful to see Aiden so happy and carefree. Perhaps…well time would tell.

A few weeks after our wedding and I still hadn't decided what I intended to do about future employment. My heart wasn't in anything I applied for and that obviously came over, as I didn't secure a single interview. In some ways I wanted a complete change. Yet, photography was still my passion so alternative work needed to include it in some respect. Bill was quite happy to have me under his feet until something suitable came along but I didn't want to get bored or become a bore. But then, one morning, the light bulb moment occurred.

After looking through our wedding photographs, I spied the other ones we took all that time ago when I first went with Bill to visit the White Lady falls. Immediately, an idea sprang to mind. I ran outside. Bill was engrossed in making a swing seat to hang in the veranda.

"I've got it," I said full of enthusiasm, holding up a photograph.

"Um, just a sec, nearly finished. Does that mean one of your photos has turned up trumps and got you an assignment," he asked casually.

"One of ours!"

I flashed the photo under his nose.

"The White Lady? Ah, well at least that job will be near home. Plus, the research is already done."

"No, not an assignment. Us, a job for us. We can start The White Lady Tours," I told him, eagerly. "People can join us for walks; we can make a display of photos we have and I'm sure they will be captured. Like the Loch Ness Monster, who won't want to try and see the White Lady?"

Bill smiled, and then laughed out loudly as he scooped me into his arms. "Do you know what? I think you are onto something. I really do."

We both started laughing with pure abandonment, slapping our thighs and shouting,

"Whoopee!"

Over the next few weeks we found out what we needed to know about starting up in business. People were fantastic, supporting and encouraging in our new venture. Aunt Bella said she would visit any time we got busy to help out. A few months previously, she had told us she had fallen in love with the area where we lived, that she was seriously thinking of moving. We hadn't told her, but Bill had already planned to renovate a ramshackle building already on site that was just ripe for improvement. Permission has been in place for a while and with a renewed application planning permission had been granted. Aunt Bella would get first refusal.

The barn, the one that used to hold Bills junk, got converted first, into a tearoom. People had fallen out of love with brown furniture and we bought several tables, for next to nothing. Once they'd had a makeover, painted cream, the tabletops sanded and oiled they looked wonderful. Chairs too came at bargain prices. With floral seat cushions, they gained a new lease of life. With lace edged tablecloths and a dresser adorned with mismatched china crockery and a vase full of wild flowers, the barn looked simply gorgeous. Down one end of the vast space, we created an area for showcasing the quilts and wall hangings I'd made. Some were traditional and others totally individual. Those I labelled myself – The chicken run; that depicted a mother hen and her chicks following across a yard outside a barn; Pretty posies, flowers from the four seasons scattered across a pink and white background. I found I was never short of ideas, just time. In fact, the more I thought about it the more I realised what an asset Aunt Bella could be.

Bill set a website up and in no time at all it was our first day of business. We got up early to make last minute preparations. I had made dozens of scones, fairy cakes and a gooey chocolate cake. We took them across to the barn. Bill looked around and smiled. "Well, we've done it. All we need now are our first customers."

"Can you fetch the packets of serviettes we bought yesterday? I forgot to bring them over."

I turned the old radio on and let out a sigh of relief. Honestly, the barn looked perfect. Nothing else needed doing. Just then Bill came lolloping across the deck, doing one of his silly walks, balancing a pile of napkins on his head!

"I've just checked the website for today and guess what? No takers, I'm afraid," he said, placing the serviettes on the counter-top.

"Well, it is the first day I suppose," I replied, sadly. "The cakes and scones will keep till tomorrow and we can always freeze them if we have to."

Then I saw a tell-tale smile creeping from Bill's mouth and the arch of one eyebrow. "You rotter. Come on, have we got a booking?"

Bill pulled me towards him and encircled me in his arms. "Have we got a booking Princess? Have we got a booking?" he repeated his voice rising to a crescendo, "We are fully booked both today and tomorrow!"

At the end of the first day we were grinning from ear to ear. Everything went so smoothly. People loved the mystical and the magical. No one was disappointed that they hadn't actually seen the White Lady. The beautiful walk to the falls more than made up for that. The idea that they just might capture a photo as we had seemed to spark interest and excitement and the cream teas at the end of their bout of exercise went down a treat. It was a wonderful day all round although, we were exhausted by the time we latched the barn door and came indoors. Yet, our tiredness was the sort you feel good about.

We fell asleep in our chairs by the fire after supper, sated and enormously satisfied that our efforts had paid off. In the evening Bailey seemed glad to get us all to himself although he hadn't been any trouble. He loved people and wanted to greet every paying customer. In anticipation of a good walk, he looked over the top of the stable door, his tongue lolling out of the side of his mouth until Bill gave him permission to join him for the trail.

I sold three quilts within the first two weeks of our business opening. We were both thrilled our decision to work for ourselves had paid off. Bill took over taking folk on walks to the falls accompanied by his loyal pal Bailey while I served cream teas. Keeping up with orders for small wall hangings and baking delicious treats took up any spare time. And, two days a week we kept for ourselves. The balance was ideal.

On our precious days off we spent time decorating the cottage. In fact we only had the small bedroom adjacent to ours to complete. We first talked of making it into a dressing room but that wasn't really us. A bit too grandiose! Aunt Bella was already happily preparing to move into the little cottage nearby that had a spare room but an extra bedroom in our home could come in useful for that unexpected guest we decided.

"Which colour do you prefer," Bill asked, the

colour chart in his hands. I took it from him and walked across to the window, to the light.

"The apple blossom pink is delicate and soft but there again, blue sky is lovely too."

"Anybody would think we are having a baby – pink or blue!" Bill chortled. Then he looked back at me and saw my eyes full of tears. "I'm sorry, so sorry," he said.

"No, don't be. I've been thinking. Remember a long time ago you mentioned adoption or fostering a child. Would you still consider that?"

"In a heartbeat."

And now, nine months later, after assessment and training, we are about to get our first foster child, a little boy, six months old. (We decorated the room in neutral colours with pale yellow accents in the end.) Physically and emotionally demanding it will be, but we are passionate about making a difference, believing The Hideaway is the perfect place in which to give a child a loving home. Who knows, we might become like the Waltons – 'Night John Boy', 'Night Mary Ellen' and 'Night night' to anyone else who wishes to share our home.

Does my life sound perfect now? Well, it is. What's more, just when I thought happiness like ours couldn't blossom outside of our patch, my brother Aiden and Julie announce their engagement.

Yes, the road to happiness isn't always the one you choose for yourself. Sometimes you get given a helping hand.

Printed in Great Britain
by Amazon

22827771R00078